"What you're actually talking about, Jed, is blackmail—

"Of the emotional kind, if nothing else," she added decisively as he would have interrupted. "Isn't it?" she prompted as his mouth thinned angrily.

His jaw tightened, his hands clenched into fists at his sides. "I'm talking about an exchange of—"

"Blackmail, Jed," Georgie insisted softly.

His eyes flashed silvery-gray. "All right, then—blackmail," he accepted tautly. "What's your answer going to be?"

Legally wed,
But he's never said…
"I love you."

They're

The series where marriages are made in
haste…and love comes later….

Look out for the next book in the *WEDLOCKED!*
miniseries on sale in December

The Christmas Baby's Gift
by Kate Walker
Harlequin Presents #2365

Carole Mortimer

BRIDE BY BLACKMAIL

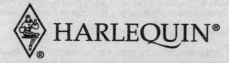

TORONTO • NEW YORK • LONDON
AMSTERDAM • PARIS • SYDNEY • HAMBURG
STOCKHOLM • ATHENS • TOKYO • MILAN • MADRID
PRAGUE • WARSAW • BUDAPEST • AUCKLAND

June,
a very good friend as well as mother-in-law.
We all miss you.

ISBN 0-373-12334-5

BRIDE BY BLACKMAIL

First North American Publication 2003.

Copyright © 2003 by Carole Mortimer.

This edition published by arrangement with Harlequin Books S.A.

® and TM are trademarks of the publisher. Trademarks indicated with ® are registered in the United States Patent and Trademark Office, the Canadian Trade Marks Office and in other countries.

Visit us at www.eHarlequin.com

Printed in U.S.A.

CHAPTER ONE

'YOU didn't mention that your parents had other guests staying this weekend,' Georgie remarked interestedly as they drove down the driveway. She could see that not only had Sukie, Andrew's older sister—by the presence of her sporty little red car—decided to pay one of her rare visits, but that there was also another car parked on the driveway next to Gerald Lawson's serviceable Range Rover. A gunmetal-grey Jaguar sports car. Very nice!

Although it was only big enough for two people, Georgie decided, which perhaps meant there wouldn't be too many other guests this weekend. Georgie had only recently become acquainted with her future in-laws—Andrew's parents and only sister—and they were quite enough to cope with for the moment: Sir Gerald and Lady Annabelle Lawson—Sir Gerald had been knighted two years ago, on his active retirement, at fifty, from politics—and Suzanna Lawson, Sukie to family and friends alike, a model.

'I wasn't aware of it myself,' Andrew answered apologetically in reply to her query. 'Could just be a—a friend of Sukie's, I suppose,' he added disparagingly. There was no love lost between brother and sister. Sukie's career as a model didn't sit too well with Andrew's more serious role as a successful lawyer. Sukie's bohemian friends didn't go down too well with him, either!

But, after the battles that had gone on in her own family over the years, Georgie considered the Lawsons quite normal by comparison!

'A successful one, by the look of the car,' Andrew continued with appreciation as he parked his black BMW next to the Jaguar. 'That will make a nice change,' he added dryly.

Georgie chuckled as she got out of the car, the gravel crunching beneath her shoes—flattish brown court, to complement the brown knee-length dress she was wearing because their time of arrival coincided with dinner.

Tall and slender, Georgie wore her red hair in a short boyishly gamine style, with wispy tendrils on her forehead and at her temples softening the severity of the style. She had clear green eyes slanted beneath auburn brows, and her nose was small and snub, with a dusting of the freckles that often accompanied such fair colouring. A peach lip-gloss softened the fullness of her mouth, and her pointed chin hinted at the determined nature beneath her smile. Stubborn contrariness, her grandfather had once called it...

Her smile faded slightly to be replaced by a perplexed frown, some of the warmth disappearing from the summer evening because of the unwelcome intrusion of thoughts about her grandfather. Though otherwise hers was a contented life.

How could she not feel contented? She had Andrew, dear, sweet, kind, *predictable* Andrew. Her first children's book was in print and doing very nicely, thank you. Her apartment was decorated and furnished to her own taste. In fact, almost everything in her life was perfectly sunny at the moment.

Which was usually the time, Georgie knew from experience, when someone decided it was time to send in a rain cloud!

'Okay, darling?' Andrew had collected their weekend bags from the boot of the car and was waiting at the bottom of the stone steps that led up to the huge front door for Georgie to join him.

'Perfect,' Georgie instantly assured him, very firmly shaking off the momentary cloud that thoughts of her grandfather had evoked. She smiled warmly at Andrew before tucking her hand into the crook of his arm.

At twenty-seven—four years older than Georgie—Andrew was six feet tall, with blond hair that occasionally fell endearingly over his brow and eyes of warm blue in a youthfully pleasant face. A couple of games of badminton a week at the gym that he frequented after work was over for the day maintained his fitness. He owed his successful career as a junior partner in a London law firm completely to the fact that he was good at his job, and not to the fact that he was Sir Gerald Lawson's son.

Andrew was everything that Georgie wanted in her future husband: pleasant-mannered, considerate, caring, and most of all even-tempered. Completely unlike—

Stop!

Unwelcome thoughts of her grandfather had been quite enough for one evening, without thinking about *him* too!

'Your parents and Miss Sukie are in the drawing room, Mr Andrew,' the butler answered in reply to Andrew's query, at the same time relieving Andrew of their luggage.

'The drawing room, no less. Not the family sitting room,' Andrew murmured ruefully as he and Georgie walked arm in arm through the wide hallway towards the formal drawing room. 'Definitely not one of Sukie's less-than-respectable friends, then,' he teased.

'Andrew!' Lady Annabelle greeted him warmly as they entered the room, standing up to rush over and hug her son. She was tiny and blonde, and still very beautiful despite being in her early fifties. Her plain black dress was a perfect foil for her delicate build and fair colouring.

Sir Gerald Lawson had risen at their entrance too, moving forward to kiss Georgie lightly on the cheek before shaking his son warmly by the hand.

An older version of Andrew, Georgie had found Gerald easy to get on with from the first. Annabelle, she was a little less sure of, she acknowledged, even as she stepped forward to accept the other woman's cool kiss on her cheek.

Although Annabelle was outwardly friendly, Georgie nevertheless sensed there was a certain reserve in her manner towards her. But, to be fair, Andrew was her only son, as well as the 'baby' of the family, and Annabelle obviously wanted the best for him. It was up to Georgie to convince the other woman that was what she was!

'Isn't it a beautiful evening?' Gerald enthused as he poured them both a pre-dinner glass of sherry. 'Almost warm enough to eat outside.'

'Don't be provincial, Gerald,' Annabelle rebuked gently. 'Besides, we have guests for dinner,' she reminded him archly.

Speaking of whom…?

What had become patently obvious to Georgie in the last few minutes was that the older Lawsons were alone in the drawing room. Which begged the question— where were Sukie and the mystery guests?

Andrew gave Georgie a conspiratorial wink before turning back to his mother. 'I noticed Sukie's car outside; where's she hiding herself?'

'Taking my name in vain again, little brother?' the recognisable voice of his sister queried as she came through from the conservatory that sided this sunlit room.

A younger version of her mother to look at, but with her father's height, Sukie was another member of the family that Georgie wasn't too sure of yet. Only a year older than Andrew, Sukie had a brittle hardness that was reflected in her cool blue eyes. The short blue dress she was wearing this evening showed off the slenderness of her figure and a long expanse of slender bare legs.

'I had no idea you were interested in flowers, Sukie,' Andrew taunted his older sister as she strolled into the room to kiss him on the cheek.

'Only the type delivered by the florist, darling,' Sukie answered him with cool dismissal. 'I was actually just showing our guest around.'

Guest, not guests. Which probably meant *she* was the other guest, Georgie realised ruefully. Oh, well, only time could change Annabelle's opinion of her. She—

Georgie gasped as the guest stepped into the room behind Sukie, the smile becoming fixed on her lips, her expression like a mask as she simply froze. Even her breathing seemed to stop momentarily as she simply stared at the man. This wasn't a rain cloud—it was a hurricane!

Named Jed Lord!

Cool, fathomless grey eyes looked across the room at her as he registered her shocked recognition. A shock that wasn't reflected in his own demeanour. Which could only mean that he had already known the two of them were to meet this evening...

Aged in his mid-thirties, he was well over six feet tall. The tailoring of his well-cut suit did nothing to hide the powerful physique beneath. He had hair as dark as night, though it was the sheer power in the hardness of his face that dominated: his grey eyes scrutinised the scene from beneath jutting black brows, and above a straight, uncompromising nose; his sculptured lips, although curved into a humourless smile at the moment, hinted at the hardness that was such an integral part of his character, and his jaw was square and determined.

Georgie, who had thought—hoped!—she'd never see him again, was completely thrown by the unexpectedness of this meeting. A fact of which Jed, so supremely self-confident as he strolled further into the room, was obviously well aware.

Damn him!

What was he *doing* here? Was he Annabelle and Gerald's guest, or had he, as Andrew and she had thought earlier when they'd arrived, come here with Sukie? The latter, Georgie noticed, was certainly looking at him like a cat about to lap up the cream!

But hadn't women always looked at Jed in that way? Hadn't *she* once? Once, perhaps, but certainly not now!

'Jed, do let me introduce you to the rest of the family.'

Gerald encouraged the other man to join them, drawing him into the circle. 'Jed Lord: my son, Andrew, and his fiancée, Georgina Jones. Although we all call her Georgie,' Gerald added warmly.

'Andrew.' Jed moved forward to shake the younger man's hand.

Georgie found she was holding her breath as he slowly turned towards her, having no idea what was going to happen in the next few minutes. Would Jed acknowledge that the two of them already knew each other? Or would he greet her as if she were a complete stranger to him?

Although hadn't she always been so, even when they should have been at their closest…?

Either way, Jed's being here, in the home of Andrew's parents, was completely disastrous to her peace of mind!

'Georgina,' Jed greeted her throatily as he stepped close to her.

She stared down at the hand he held out to her, a long tapered hand with a masculine beauty that totally belied its strength. How could she possibly shake it when she didn't even want to touch him? It was—

'Or may I call you Georgie…?' he prompted huskily, that grey gaze intent on the paleness of her face as she still made no effort to take the hand he held out to her.

Almost like a peace offering. Except there could never be any sort of peace between Jed and herself!

'Of course,' Georgie accepted vaguely, forcing herself to brush her fingers lightly against his, a shiver running icily down her spine even as she snatched her hand away before his fingers could curl around hers. Just that brief touch had been enough to tell her that she still couldn't bear to be anywhere near this man!

'Dinner is served, Sir Gerald,' the butler announced politely.

'Thank you, Bancroft,' his employer rejoined cheerfully. 'Shall we go through to the dining room?' he suggested lightly.

Dinner. There was no way that Georgie could eat. No way she could possibly sit down at the same dinner table as Jed Lord!

Except... What choice did she have? Like her, Jed had given no indication that the two of them already knew each other. She knew her own reasons for not doing so, but she had no idea what Jed's were for the lack of disclosure on his part. But one thing she did know about Jed, though—they would be his own reasons, and no one else's. Because Jed never did anything that wasn't to his own liking.

'May I?' Gerald held out his arm to escort her in to dinner.

Well, at least she wasn't expected to go through to dinner as Jed's partner; that would have been more than she could stand. In fact, she wasn't sure how she was still standing at all after the shock she had received!

'Thank you.' She took Gerald's arm, noting that Sukie had laid a firm claim on Jed, her long red-painted nails on his hand as she moved in close to him, while Andrew was left to escort his mother.

But Georgie was completely aware of Jed walking behind her as they went through to the dining room, could feel the heat of his gaze on her back. That enig-

matic grey gaze that could freeze with coldness or bur.
with desire…!

But more often freeze with coldness, she reminded
herself hollowly.

She had been so looking forward to this weekend in
the Hampshire countryside with Andrew; the Lawson
family home edged the New Forest. But with Jed here
it had turned into a nightmare from which she couldn't
seem to wake!

To make matters worse, Jed sat opposite her at the
oval dining table. Although it would have been even
more unbearable if he had sat next to her. The simple
truth was he shouldn't be there at all!

She looked at him from beneath lowered auburn
lashes as their first course was served to them. He looked
much the same as when she had last seen him a year
ago, although there were perhaps more lines beside his
eyes and mouth, and a faint dusting of grey amongst the
black hair at his temples. Although that, she acknowledged disgustedly, only made him look more devilishly
attractive!

'Is the smoked salmon not to your liking, Georgie?'
Jed remarked mildly. 'You aren't eating,' he pointed out
as she gave him a startled look.

She could feel the colour warm her cheeks at having
attention drawn to her in this way. Deliberately so, she
was sure. One look at the mocking amusement in Jed's
eyes was enough to tell her he was enjoying himself. At
her expense.

What else? Jed had been laughing at her most of her
life, it seemed to her. But it was time it stopped!

She gave him a brightly false smile. 'You know, Mr

Lord, I love smoked salmon.' She picked up her knife and fork and began to eat.

'Please, do call me Jed,' he invited dryly, grey gaze assessing.

'Such an unusual name,' Annabelle remarked lightly.

'Isn't it?' Georgie agreed, turning back to Jed, the light of challenge in her own gaze now. 'Surely it must be the diminutive of something else…?' She looked at Jed expectantly.

His gaze hardened and his mouth twisted into a grimace. 'Jeremiah,' he supplied tersely.

'Goodness me!' Georgie laughed softly, easily holding his warning grey stare with her own clear green eyes. 'No wonder you prefer Jed.'

'That's a little unkind to our guest, Georgie.' Annabelle Lawson shot her a reproving glance.

'As it happens, Annabelle,' Jed turned to his hostess, smiling wryly, 'I wholeheartedly agree with Georgie!'

That must be a first, Georgie acknowledged ruefully. Still, at least she had proved—to herself, if no one else!—that this evening didn't have to go all Jed's way!

'I wasn't meaning to be rude, Mr Lord,' she assured him, although she was sure Jed, at least, didn't miss the edge of derision in her tone. 'It was just a comment on the names some parents expect their children to live with!'

'Your own, for example,' Jed came back softly.

'*Touché.*' She gave an acknowledging inclination of her head; she should have known she wouldn't have the last word! She never had where Jed was concerned. 'I was named for my grandfather,' she said determinedly.

Jed raised dark brows. 'You have a grandfather called Georgina?'

'I—' Georgie broke off her sharp response as Sukie, seated beside Jed, gave a shout of laughter.

Really—Jed's joke hadn't been *that* funny, Georgie decided irritably as Sukie continued to chuckle.

'I think you rather asked for that one, darling.' Andrew, seated on Georgie's left, lightly covered Georgie's hand with his own as he smiled at her indulgently.

Possibly, she inwardly conceded. But it really hadn't been that funny. She could—

Jed was looking at Andrew's hand, which still rested on Georgie's, his forehead furrowed over hard eyes.

What on earth—?

'The emerald of your engagement ring is the same colour as your eyes,' Jed bit out unexpectedly.

That was exactly what Andrew had said to her the day they had visited a jewellers to choose it!

But she didn't for a moment think that Jed meant it in the romantic way that Andrew had that day. She could clearly hear the accusation in Jed's tone, even if no one else could.

'When is the wedding?' Jed's icy gaze moved from the ring to Georgie's face, although his closed expression gave away none of his thoughts.

Had it ever? Georgie acknowledged disgustedly before answering him tersely, 'Next Easter.'

His mouth quirked wryly. 'Such a long time away...' he remarked enigmatically.

Georgie gave him a sharp glance. Exactly what did he mean by that? Impossible to tell; his expression exactly matched his tone of voice. But he had meant something. She had known Jed long enough to know he was a man of few words, and the ones he did choose to say always had meaning.

'We have our hearts set on an Easter wedding.' Andrew was the one to answer Jed, squeezing Georgie's hand reassuringly as he did so. 'Are you a married man yourself, Jed?' he asked interestedly.

Georgie suddenly found she was holding her breath as she waited for Jed's reply.

His mouth tightened. 'Not any more,' he finally answered slowly. 'I recently entered the statistics of divorced men,' he added with humour.

'How sad,' Annabelle put in sympathetically.

Jed turned to smile at the older woman. 'Thank you, Annabelle, but I doubt my ex-wife thinks so! She was the one to divorce me,' he enlarged bitterly.

'What a very silly woman,' Sukie put in throatily, her blue eyes full of invitation as she looked flirtatiously at Jed from beneath lowered lashes.

'Not at all,' Jed dismissed, picking up his glass to sip the white wine that had been poured to accompany their salmon. 'The grounds for divorce were typical—my wife understood me!' he drawled sardonically.

'Shouldn't that be, 'My wife *didn't* understand me'?' prompted a perplexed Annabelle, obviously not at all happy with the slant the conversation had suddenly taken at her dinner table.

Which wasn't surprising, Georgie acknowledged impatiently. Jed Lord's divorce—for whatever reason!—was hardly appropriate dinner conversation anywhere!

'No, Annabelle, I do believe I had it right the first time,' Jed replied meaningfully.

'How absolutely priceless!' Sukie was the one to answer now as she chuckled throatily. 'Were you a very naughty boy, Jed?' she prompted with amusement.

He shrugged broad shoulders. 'My wife obviously thought so, otherwise she wouldn't have divorced me.'

'Do eat some more of your salmon, Jed,' Annabelle encouraged nervously. 'I believe you've recently spent some time in America, do tell us about it?'

Which was Annabelle's way of firmly saying that was the end of that particular subject.

Which was probably as well, Georgie thought as she determinedly focused her attention again on her plate of smoked salmon. The murmur of voices around the table were now passing her by completely. If Jed had said one more word about the wife who had divorced him because she understood him, she might not have been able to stop herself from standing up and hitting him!

Because, until six months ago, *she* had been his wife!

CHAPTER TWO

'YOU were very quiet during dinner, darling; are you feeling all right?' Andrew asked concernedly once the party had moved back into the drawing room after their meal, to enjoy coffee and liqueurs.

Georgie moved closer to him as he sat down beside her on the sofa, studiously avoiding looking across the room to where Jed and Sukie stood talking together softly. 'I'm feeling fine,' she assured Andrew. 'A slight headache, that's all. I'll be fine after a good night's sleep.'

Although she wasn't sure, with Jed in the same house, that she would be able to get the latter at all! But just to be away from his oppressive company would be something!

'What do you think of Jed Lord?' Andrew prompted, seeming to pick up on at least the subject of her thoughts, and glancing consideringly across the room at the other man.

If she were to tell Andrew, here and now, exactly what she thought of Jed Lord then he would probably be extremely shocked. But she accepted that after tonight she would have to talk to Andrew about Jed at some time in the near future.

So far in their five-month relationship she had put off telling Andrew that, at only twenty-three, she had already been married and divorced. At first it hadn't seemed the sort of thing you just confided to a relative stranger, and then as they'd got to know each other, to love each other, it still hadn't been something she felt she could just baldly state as a fact.

But with Jed's appearance in the Lawson home she realised she wouldn't be able to put it off for much longer. In fact, she was surprised that the troublemaking Jed Lord she had known of old hadn't already just blurted out that she was the ex-wife about whom he had been talking over dinner. If only to watch her squirm!

But he hadn't. Which meant he must have his own reasons for not doing so...

No wonder she had a headache!

'Think of him?' she answered Andrew brightly. 'In what way?'

'In any way,' Andrew replied. 'Sukie certainly seems to find him fascinating—and my big sister isn't easily impressed!'

No, she wasn't. But then Sukie didn't know Jed in the way that Georgie knew him, and obviously found his dark, brooding good-looks and arrogant self-assurance extremely attractive. So had Georgie once...

'I doubt she would have brought him here with her if she wasn't.' Georgie evaded answering Andrew's question directly.

'Oh, Jed Lord didn't come down with Sukie. My father told me over dinner that he's a business acquaintance of his,' Andrew confided.

Georgie looked frowningly at Jed. Gerald Lawson, since his retirement from politics, had returned to his earlier business interests. But as far as she was aware they didn't include hotels, which she knew was where Jed's family business concerns lay.

'Really?' she murmured contemplatively. 'In that case, Sukie is certainly a fast worker,' she added dryly as Andrew's sister all but draped herself across Jed as they talked.

Andrew gave a disgusted snort. 'She's wasting her time with a man like Jed Lord.'

Georgie gave him a quizzical frown. 'What do you mean…?'

'From what's been said, the man has only just escaped from one disastrous relationship—I seriously doubt he intends embarking on another. And he's experienced enough to realise my big sister is trouble with a capital T!' Andrew dismissed scornfully.

Georgie gave a wry shake of her head. 'He doesn't give the impression that he's a man who runs away from trouble.' In fact, she knew he wasn't! 'Besides, Andrew—' she turned to him teasingly, deciding they had talked about Jed Lord quite enough for one evening '—when did you become so knowledgeable about experienced men?' She gave him a mischievous smile.

Andrew smiled. 'I'm twenty-seven, Georgie, not seven!' he returned.

This was what she liked about being with Andrew: the complete freedom to do and say whatever she liked without fear of offending or angering him. Andrew was so easy-going she was totally relaxed in his company.

Something she had never been in Jed's!

She frowned as she remembered her response earlier to the brief brush of Jed's hand against hers when they were introduced. She had thought she was completely over him, that the finality of their divorce six months previously had severed all emotional ties to him. But, to her chagrin, she had felt more than just loathing earlier at his touch...

'Hey, I was only joking, Georgie,' Andrew chided softly, misunderstanding the reason for her frown. 'I've never pretended to be an innocent, but neither am I a man of experience myself.' He gave a rueful shake of his head. 'I've been too busy making a successful career for myself to have too much time for that sort of thing.'

'You don't mind that the wedding isn't until next Easter?' she said concernedly, knowing that it had been her decision that they wait; she hadn't told Andrew so, but she wanted time to make sure she didn't make yet another mistake in her life. Although she was already pretty sure that Andrew would never let her down. Unlike— 'I just thought an Easter wedding would be nice,' she added warmly. Especially as her wedding to Jed had taken place at Christmas!

She still cringed at how young and naïve she had been then. How trusting. How utterly, utterly stupid!

'And it will be.' Andrew hugged her reassuringly. 'We—'

'I hope you don't mind if we interrupt you two love-birds?' interrupted a sarcastic, familiar voice.

Georgie stiffened at the sound of Jed's voice, glancing up reluctantly to see that he and Sukie were beside the sofa. Sukie looked no more pleased than Georgie. Obviously it had been Jed's decision to come over...

Georgie looked up at him challengingly, his sarcasm not lost on her even if it was on Andrew and Sukie. Hard grey eyes returned her interest, that sculptured face set into uncompromising lines. It wasn't hard to guess, after his reference to 'love-birds', just why he was looking so grim.

But it was no longer any of Jed's business who she showed her affection to. If it ever had been! Besides, Andrew was her fiancé, the man she was going to marry.

'Please do,' she answered smoothly, at the same time deciding to stand up; she did not intend giving Jed any sort of advantage over her!

Petty, perhaps, but that was the level to which their relationship had deteriorated before that final big blow-up.

Andrew stood at her side, his arm moving lightly about the slenderness of her waist. 'My father tells me that your family are in hotels, Jed,' he prompted with polite interest.

'Yes,' Jed answered the other man abruptly while his eyes continued to rest on Georgie.

Georgie, who was becoming more and more uncomfortable by the second, was aware that Jed, a man who had never particularly cared for the social niceties before, was now behaving very rudely by continuing to stare at her. In the same way that their brief conversation at dinner hadn't been socially polite either. If he didn't start behaving in a more circumspect way someone in the Lawson family—probably the more astute Sukie—was going to guess that they weren't complete strangers after all.

'That must be very interesting,' she put in lightly, her expression warning as Jed looked at her.

'It can be.' His answer was maddeningly unforthcoming.

Like getting blood out of a stone!

Like trying to find a heart somewhere in that stone...

'You're an author, I believe, Georgie.' He spoke mildly.

'Yes,' she confirmed warily.

'Will I have seen one of your books in the shops?' He continued his line of questioning.

Her mouth tightened. 'Not unless your taste runs to children's books, no,' she bit out tautly, wondering exactly where this conversation was going. Or if, indeed, it was going anywhere!

One thing she did know just from looking at Jed's face: he had already known what her answer was going to be—if not quite prepared for the way in which she gave it!

So he already knew that she had written and had published a book for children...

How had he known that? There had been no personal contact of any kind between the two of them for over a year now, all correspondence concerning their divorce having passed between their two lawyers. And Georgie had deliberately avoided seeing anyone who might have contact with Jed.

But, nevertheless, she had no doubt that Jed already knew everything there was to know about the book she had written...

Jed's mouth quirked. 'I'm afraid not. Still, it's an— unusual career,' he added softly.

'What's unusual about it?' Georgie prompted sharply, on the defensive as she glared at him.

He shrugged broad shoulders. 'Perhaps it's only that I've never met an author before.'

That wasn't what he'd meant at all—and they both knew it. Even if no one else in the room did...

'Yes, I'm very proud of Georgie.' Andrew spoke warmly, giving her waist a reassuring squeeze as he smiled down at her.

'And what about you, Georgie?' Jed spoke hardly. 'Are you proud of your achievement?'

'Of course,' she answered him stiffly.

He gave an acknowledging inclination of his head. 'Is it something you've always wanted to do? Or—?'

'Would you care for another brandy, Jed?' Sukie cut in firmly, obviously intending to change the subject, not at all happy that the conversation was focused on Georgie.

Which was perfectly okay with Georgie—she wasn't happy about it either!

'No, thanks.' Jed answered Sukie dismissively, not even glancing her way as he did so. 'Have you always known you wanted to be an author, Georgie?'

Her eyes narrowed on him warningly. He knew damn well she hadn't always wanted to be an author, that until two years ago her only ambition had been to be his wife, to spend the rest of her life with him.

Which, in retrospect, was no ambition at all!

'I've always known I wanted to be something,' she replied with firm dismissal. 'It seems I've been lucky enough to find a career that I not only like but which one publisher at least thinks I'm good at.' That knowledge still gave her an inner warm glow.

'How do you feel about having a working wife, Andrew?' Jed looked at the younger man mockingly.

'I feel absolutely fine about it,' Andrew came back,

sounding perplexed. 'Most women want a career of their own nowadays—to be more than just some man's wife.'

'Do they?' Jed murmured softly.

'Of course we do.' Sukie was the one to answer lightly, linking her arm with Jed's. 'Maybe that's where you went wrong, Jed,' she added teasingly.

Jed continued to look at Georgie for several long minutes, before he straightened and turned to Sukie, his smile wry. 'Maybe it was,' he murmured in agreement. 'Although, listening to my wife, I would be hard pushed to find anything I did right!'

'Ex-wife,' Georgie heard herself correct, heated colour entering her cheeks when she realised—as Sukie and Andrew had no idea of her past relationship with Jed! To them she probably sounded as if she was being rude again.

'I stand corrected.' Jed gave an acknowledging nod of his head, lips curved into a humourless smile as he dared her to add to that admission.

It was a challenge she had no intention of taking him up on—they had talked about Jed Lord and his defunct marriage far too much already this evening as far as she was concerned!

'Are you staying the whole weekend, Mr—Jed?' She corrected herself before he could do it for her. 'It's a beautiful area. I'm sure Sukie would love to show you some of the surrounding countryside.' She received a grateful smile from her future sister-in-law at this suggestion.

'You're right; it is a beautiful area,' Jed drawled dryly. 'Unfortunately, I'm leaving in the morning.'

Unfortunate for whom? Georgie's raised eyebrows

conveyed her amusement. Certainly not for her; she couldn't wait to see the back of him!

Also, she couldn't believe he was enjoying this encounter any more than she was; the two of them had made their opinions of each other more than plain the last time they had spoken at length together.

'What a pity,' she answered, completely disingenuous.

'Isn't it?' he came back, with the same insincerity, laughter crinkling the lines around his eyes as he met her gaze.

Georgie drew in a sharp breath, knowing that the two of them weren't behaving very well. They really were going to arouse suspicion if they didn't stop this verbal fencing—right now!

She turned to Andrew, her hand resting lightly on his arm. 'Shall we go and make our excuses to your parents now, darling?' she suggested. 'We've both had a busy week, and I'm sure you must be tired after driving down here.'

Andrew brightened at her obvious concern, making Georgie feel doubly guilty. Firstly, because she knew her desire to escape to the privacy of her bedroom had nothing to do with concern for Andrew, and secondly, because she knew how upset and confused Andrew would feel if he knew it had everything to do with getting away from Jed Lord!

'I hope you'll excuse us, Jed?' Andrew said politely. 'It's been a great pleasure meeting you,' he added warmly, shaking the other man's hand before putting his arm firmly about Georgie's waist to steer her across the room to where his parents sat, softly conversing together.

'"A great pleasure" meeting him?' she muttered to Andrew sceptically.

He gave her waist a light squeeze. 'I'll explain later,' he promised.

Having made her excuses to Andrew's parents, Georgie could once again feel Jed's piercing grey gaze burning into her back as she walked to the door, knowing her movements lacked their normal graceful fluidity, but unable to do anything about it. She wouldn't be able to relax again completely until she was safely away from Jed. Make that until Jed was far, far away from the Lawson home!

Although she did breathe a little easier once she and Andrew were outside in the hallway.

She was grateful for the fact that Jed hadn't given away their previous connection, but at the same time she questioned why he hadn't. It certainly couldn't have been to save any embarrassment on her part; Jed just didn't work that way.

'You didn't enjoy this evening, did you?' Andrew enquired ruefully, his head tilted as he looked down at her questioningly.

Georgie looked up at him quizzically. 'Whatever makes you think that?' she delayed.

Had she and Jed given themselves away after all? It wouldn't be so surprising if they had; they certainly hadn't spoken to each other like people who had just been introduced...

Andrew laughed softly. 'I know, from personal experience, that my family is enough to cope with without someone like Jed Lord thrown in for good measure!'

She frowned. 'I had the impression a few minutes ago that you actually liked the man.'

Andrew grinned. 'That was the impression I intended giving.'

Georgie still frowned, not altogether sure she was happy with this explanation. She hadn't believed Andrew capable of subterfuge, but his explanation now gave a different impression completely...

'But why?' Her expression showed complete confusion.

Andrew elaborated as they continued to make their way up the stairs. 'My father owns some land that the L & J Group is interested in purchasing for yet another of their luxury hotels. You've heard of the L & J Group, haven't you?'

Heard of them—she had once been part of them!

'Hasn't everyone?' she dismissed dryly.

'Hmm,' Andrew sighed. 'Anyway, Dad's playing hard-to-get with this piece of land,' he explained.

'Good for him!' Georgie came back vehemently. A little too vehemently, she realised, as Andrew looked at her in surprise. 'Sorry.' She grimaced. 'But even on such short acquaintance I got the impression that Mr Jeremiah Lord is a little too fond of having his own way.'

Andrew nodded slowly. 'He does give that impression, doesn't he? Makes you almost feel sorry for his ex-wife, doesn't it?'

Once again Georgie gave him a frowning look. 'Only almost...?'

'Well—he isn't my type, you understand,' Andrew replied, 'but I got the distinct impression from Sukie's behaviour towards him that Jed Lord is rather attractive to women.'

It would have been impossible to miss Sukie's interest in Jed! 'I didn't find him in the least attractive!' Georgie exclaimed forcefully.

'I know,' Andrew agreed. 'Actually, darling, it might have been a little more politically correct—for the sake of father's business deal, you understand?—if you hadn't shown your dislike of the man quite so openly.'

Her eyes widened at the unexpected rebuke. 'I can't be less than I am, Andrew,' she responded. 'And being pleasant to a man I dislike is not—'

'Don't take it all so seriously, Georgie!' Andrew cut in teasingly, obviously realising he had gone too far. 'I love you just the way you are.'

Georgie looked up at him uncertainly in the dimmed lighting of the hallway. 'I love you too, Andrew,' she told him uncertainly.

'That's all that matters, then, isn't it?' he murmured, before kissing her.

For a brief moment Georgie froze, still thrown by Andrew's sycophantic attitude towards Jed a few minutes ago. Not only that, Andrew had actually criticised her for her behaviour towards the man!

But as Andrew continued to kiss her the anger she felt towards him began to evaporate, and she kissed him back with a fierceness that bordered on desperation, knowing that the last thing she needed at this moment was to feel less than sure of the feelings she and Andrew had for each other.

'Wow!' he murmured a few minutes later as they broke their embrace, his forehead resting lightly on hers as he looked at her. 'Perhaps we shouldn't wait until next Easter to get married, after all?' he urged huskily.

No! Yes! Georgie was no longer sure about anything at this moment... Part of her wanted to marry Andrew tomorrow. But another part of her knew that, no matter how she might try to shut it out, Andrew's attitude towards Jed, even if it was purely a business manouevre, still bothered her. For a start, it didn't seem characteristic of the Andrew she'd thought she knew...

She was also aware that it was seeing Jed Lord again that was making her have doubts about waiting until Easter to marry Andrew...

'If it takes you this long to think about it...'

Georgie's frown deepened. Andrew sounded almost sulky...

'I was only joking, Georgie,' Andrew assured her as he saw the consternation on her face. 'An Easter wedding is fine with me. Which reminds me. We really should start doing something towards making plans in that direction. My mother tells me that it takes months to arrange a wedding.'

Maybe it did, to arrange a church wedding, with hundreds of guests invited and a huge reception afterwards at a fashionable venue. But, as a divorced woman, Georgie knew that wasn't the sort of wedding she and Andrew were likely to have. Something else she really needed to discuss with him...

But not now. She needed to get this weekend over with first, then she and Andrew could sit down and talk about their future together. Including what sort of wedding they were going to have and who the wedding guests were likely to be. The fact that she didn't want to invite one single member of her family was definitely going to be cause for discussion!

Oh, Andrew knew that both her parents were dead, and that she had been brought up by her grandfather. But he wasn't a subject she had discussed in any great detail either. Andrew had seemed to accept her reticence, but Georgie wasn't as sure Annabelle Lawson was going to be so agreeable about it. Especially when the other woman learned exactly who Georgie's grandfather was!

'If you're really sure about waiting, we still have plenty of time for all that,' she soothed.

Andrew looked at her searchingly. 'All this discussion about divorce hasn't put you off, has it?' he asked.

In all honesty, it wasn't talk of divorce that had suddenly made her feel less than certain about her wedding to Andrew; it was this other side of her fiancé that she had never seen before.

Nevertheless, her mouth firmed as she recalled exactly whose divorce had been discussed this evening. 'Not in the least,' she answered. 'You are absolutely nothing like Jed Lord,' she added with certainty. That was one thing she was sure of; she wouldn't be attracted to Andrew if he were anything like Jed Lord! 'I can all too easily imagine why his wife wanted to get away from him!'

Andrew looked concerned. 'You really didn't like him, did you?'

'No,' she confirmed with an inward shudder. Jed wasn't a man who was easy to like; you either loved him or hated him. And Georgie knew which emotion she felt towards him!

'Oh, well, with any luck you may not have to meet him again,' Andrew said. 'I don't think my father will keep him waiting too much longer for an answer on that land.'

Georgie looked at him searchingly. 'Is everything all right? With your father, I mean?' If it wasn't, maybe that would explain the difference she had sensed in Andrew's manner earlier?

Of course,' Andrew dismissed. 'Now, it's time we both went to bed, young lady; I for one am absolutely bushed.' His words were followed by an involuntary yawn. 'See.'

Georgie shook off her earlier mood of uncertainty as she smiled at him; it was probably seeing Jed again that had given her these misgivings! 'I'll see you in the morning, then.'

Andrew nodded. 'But let's not make it too early, hmm?' he ventured, sounding tired.

'As late as you like,' Georgie assured him.

With any luck Jed would already have left the next morning by the time she put in an appearance.

She could always hope!

CHAPTER THREE

'LAWSON has absolutely no idea you were once married to me, does he?'

Georgie froze in the doorway of the bathroom that adjoined her bedroom, staring across to where Jed reclined on the bed—her bed!—still dressed in the dark suit and white shirt he had worn for dinner, his head resting back on the raised pillows as he calmly returned her startled gaze.

Georgie could feel the anger building within her, was absolutely furious at finding him here, incredulous that he could have dared—have dared—

But why should she be surprised by anything Jed chose to do—hadn't he always done exactly as he pleased?

Of course he had. And he would see no problem now in invading the privacy of the bedroom allotted to her by Annabelle Lawson if that was what he chose to do. Georgie should have known she had escaped too easily earlier!

Georgie stepped further into the room, relieved she had put on her nightgown and robe after taking her shower. Although she doubted that if she had been stark naked it would have bothered Jed unduly. After all, he had seen it all before, hadn't she.

'Get out,' she told him in a coldly even tone.

Being Jed, he didn't move. 'Exactly when are you

33

going to tell Lawson about me?' he demanded scornfully. 'Before the wedding, one hopes,' he added mockingly.

'I don't happen to think that is any of your business,' Georgie responded icily.

'No?'

'No!' she confirmed shortly. 'I believe I told you to get out,' she then reminded him forcefully, all too aware of how alone they were in the privacy of her bedroom.

'I believe you did,' Jed confirmed, still making no effort to move. 'Expecting Lawson, are you?' he continued scathingly, eyeing the pale peach-coloured silk robe and nightgown she wore.

Georgie drew in a sharp breath, her body feeling suddenly warm under the onslaught of that assessing gaze. 'Again, I don't happen to think that is any of your business,' she snapped.

Jed shrugged, sitting up to swing his legs over the side of the bed, his sheer size suddenly dominating the room. 'Maybe you don't,' he conceded hardly. 'But I do.'

Her eyes widened. 'You—'

'You're looking good, Georgie.' Jed cut in huskily on her angry rebuke, grey eyes moving slowly over her, from the top of her fiery head to her size four feet. 'Very good,' he amended appreciatively.

Georgie's cheeks were as fiery red as her hair by the time that caressing grey gaze returned to her face.

How did he manage to do that? To make her completely aware, not only of the forceful attraction of his body but also her own body's response to it? Her skin seemed to burn beneath the silk material, her nipples were taut and pouting, and there was a warm glow at her thighs.

'*You* look awful,' she returned bluntly.

If not exactly truthfully. Jed did look older, there were lines beside his nose and mouth that hadn't been there a year ago, and now there were flecks of grey threaded into his almost black hair, too. But none of those things detracted from the fact that he was extremely attractive—he'd always been!

And probably always would be, she conceded wearily. Jed was not only a very handsome man, his hard features seeming as if they were carved from granite, his body lithe and fit, but he also exuded a strength, an arrogance, that would always be attractive to women, no matter what his age.

Some women, Georgie amended forcefully. She—thank goodness!—had been irrevocably cured of her own attraction towards him!

His mouth twisted ruefully at her deliberate insult. 'I see you're still as truthfully honest as ever,' he drawled. 'At least as far as I'm concerned,' he continued pointedly.

Back to the subject of her honesty with Andrew about her previous marriage...!

'And you, I see, are still as dogmatic as ever,' she returned scathingly, not rising to his challenge. 'What do you want, Jed?' she prompted sharply.

He shook his head slowly. 'I'm not sure you want to hear that,' he murmured softly.

Georgie's head snapped up. His eyes were now a deep gunmetal-grey, and a nerve was pulsing in his squarely set jaw. What—?

She took an involuntary step backwards as Jed stood up, her eyes blazing deeply green as she saw his look of speculation at her obvious response.

'Not as self-possessed as you would like me to believe, are you?' he observed with lazy satisfaction.

'Even a fox knows when to be frightened of the hound!' Georgie shot back insultingly.

Angry colour darkened his cheeks. 'Frightened?' he echoed harshly. 'You've made it more than obvious—on several occasions!—that you hate me, Georgie. But fear…?'

'Wary, then,' she amended wearily. 'Jed, it's late, and I—'

'Frightened was the word you used,' he persisted hardly.

Maybe because frightened was the right word! Five years ago, as an inexperienced eighteen-year-old, she had been frightened of the intensity of her own feelings towards this man—had sometimes felt that she couldn't breathe for loving him. Becoming his wife had only intensified those feelings, until at times she'd felt as if she was being totally consumed by him, that her own personality was becoming totally melded with his…!

'So it was,' she acknowledged lightly. 'But, as I said, it's late, and perhaps I used the word unwisely.' She sighed heavily. 'It was—a shock, finding you here this evening, Jed. Perhaps if I had known—'

'You would have found an excuse not to be here!' Jed finished for her, laughing softly as he saw more guilty colour enter her cheeks. 'Don't try to deny it, Georgie, I know you too well to be fooled by the lie. Or did you think I didn't know exactly how you would react if you had known I was to be a guest at the Lawson home this evening?'

Her eyes widened. 'So you *did* know I was going to be here?' she said slowly. She hadn't been wrong, then, in her feeling earlier that Jed had been in no way as surprised to see her this evening as she had to see him?

Jed seemed unconcerned. 'You're a very difficult woman to track down.'

Georgie was taken aback. His words had been 'track her down'. But why? What possible reason could he have for—?

'My grandfather sent you, didn't he?' she realised quickly, her spine stiffening in instinctive defence.

Jed eyed her coldly. 'Nobody sent me, Georgie,' he rasped harshly.

Of course not; Jed wouldn't allow himself to be anyone's errand boy!

'Asked you to find me, then,' she corrected impatiently. 'But it amounts to the same thing, doesn't it?'

Jed's eyes were narrowed to icy slits. 'Your grandfather has no idea that I intended seeing you this weekend,' he bit out coldly.

That didn't exactly answer her accusation, did it…?

She shrugged, turning away to toy absently with a china shepherdess that adorned the dressing table. 'In what way was I difficult to track down?' she asked.

But she already knew the answer to that. She lived in a secure apartment building, where the doorman had firm instructions not to allow any of the Lord or Jones family admittance; her telephone number was ex-directory, and as she worked from home there was no office where she could be contacted either. But she had arranged her life in that way for a purpose.

A purpose that had been rendered completely null and void by Jed's unexpected presence at the Lawson home this weekend!

'I'm sure you already know the answer to that, Georgie,' Jed replied. 'It was only the announcement of your engagement last month in *The Times* newspaper that gave us any idea of your present whereabouts,' he explained grimly.

An announcement that had been put in the newspaper by Annabelle Lawson, the other woman having firmly assured Georgie that it was social etiquette for her son's engagement to be publicly announced in this way.

'You didn't waste much time after the divorce, did you?' Jed accused.

Georgie looked at him sharply. 'I don't think my personal life is any of your business, Jed—'

'Until six months ago your personal life was completely my business!' he came back angrily, that nerve once again pulsating in his jaw.

'And now it isn't,' Georgie reminded him. 'Just say what you want to say, Jed, and then leave, hmm?' she prompted bluntly. 'It's been a long week.' And an even longer evening! 'I would like to get some sleep now.'

He stepped back from the bed. 'Don't let me stop you,' he said.

She sighed her impatience. 'You and I both know that I have no intention of getting into bed until you are out of my bedroom!'

'Why not?' he queried softly.

Her cheeks coloured hotly at his deliberate probing. 'You know why not!'

'Because you and I once shared a bed as husband and wife?' Jed's face had hardened angrily. 'You're a beautiful woman, Georgie, perhaps even more so now than you were a year ago. But I'm really not so desperate for a female to share my bed that I need to force my attentions on a woman who has claimed—more than once!—to hate me!'

'Especially when there's one just down the hallway who so obviously doesn't feel the same way!' she came back heatedly.

Jed became very still, his expression unreadable now. 'You're referring to Sukie Lawson?' he said slowly.

'Of course,' Georgie snapped. 'Although Annabelle doesn't seem impervious to your charms either,' she commented scathingly as she remembered the way the older woman had lightly flirted with Jed during dinner.

He shook his head. 'That's your future mother-in-law you're talking about.'

'She's still a woman, isn't she?' Georgie scorned. 'And you—' She broke off, completely dazed as she realised she was resorting to the sort of arguments that had peppered their three year marriage.

'Georgie—'

'Forget I said that, Jed,' she cut in quickly, disgusted with herself—and Jed!—for allowing the conversation to deteriorate in this way. 'As I said, it's been a shock seeing you here this evening,' she said in a calmer voice. 'But that's no reason for me to be insulting.'

'My, my, you have grown up,' he mocked.

Georgie ignored the taunt. 'You said earlier, or implied—' she corrected ruefully '—that you've been trying to contact me... I've had the final decree through for our divorce, so it can't be anything to do with that.' And those papers, signed, sealed, and legally verified, were very securely locked away in the safe at her apartment.

'No, it's nothing to do with the divorce,' Jed conceded. 'As you say, that is definitely final. But there is a problem. A family problem,' he went on.

Georgie froze, her hands clenching into fists at her sides as she tensed. 'My grandfather—?'

'No, not your grandfather,' Jed interrupted her harshly. 'I have no idea what the rift that exists between the two of you is about, but he, it seems, knows better than to ask you for anything!' he concluded disgustedly.

Georgie was well aware that his disgust was levelled at her...

And maybe on the face of it that feeling was justified. Her grandfather had brought her up after her parents, his only son and his daughter-in-law, had both been killed in a skiing accident when Georgie was only five.

At sixty years of age, George might have been thought to be well past the age of wanting to be bothered by such a responsibility, and might quite easily have paid for a full-time nanny for the little girl, followed by boarding-school when she was old enough. But George had done neither of those things. He had taken Georgie into his home, becoming father as well as mother to her, and taking her with him on his business travels whenever she didn't have to be at school.

As a young child Georgie had absolutely adored him, knowing that behind the forbidding façade he presented to the world in general there was a softer, more caring man. Whatever love he'd had, he'd generously given to her.

She could have had no idea then that she was just part of a grand plan...!

She scowled. 'Then what makes you think you could possibly succeed where my grandfather wouldn't even try?' she challenged Jed.

'Because, no matter what your differences were with your grandfather, I know you have always loved my grandmother,' he answered.

Georgie frowned. 'Grandie? What does she have to do with this?' Whatever 'this' was!

'Everything,' Jed answered flatly, his expression grim. 'She had a heart attack three weeks ago—'

'Grandie did?' Georgie echoed sharply, feeling a sinking feeling in her stomach that had nothing to do with her loss of appetite earlier. 'Why didn't anyone let me know? What—?'

'You've refused to see any of us except in the presence of a lawyer, remember?' Jed replied bitterly.

Her cheeks coloured at the rebuke. 'Yes, but—'

'No buts, Georgie,' Jed rasped harshly. 'You can't have it all your own way, you know. You've made it more than obvious that you want nothing more to do with the family. More to the point that you want them to have nothing more to do with you.'

Georgie couldn't quite meet that icily accusing grey gaze, knowing that what he said was true. But she had her own reasons for making that decision. Reasons that hadn't allowed for the illness of the one person in the family that she still adored...

'How is Grandie now? Is she all right?' Georgie asked agitatedly.

'Do you care?' Jed scoffed.

Her eyes flashed deeply green. 'Of course I care!' she responded angrily.

Jed gave a brief nod of his head. 'That's something, I suppose,' he allowed. 'Grandie is— She's—changed,' he finally said reluctantly. 'She wants to see you.'

Again this was typical Jed. No 'will you?', no 'could you?', no 'would you?'. Just that single bald statement.

Georgie moistened dry lips. 'When?'

'Well, not tonight, obviously,' he drawled with a sweepingly appraising glance over her night attire.

'Obviously,' she echoed, hoping that none of her inner panic at the mere thought of what was being asked of her was apparent on her face.

Her break with the family two years ago had been irrevocable, final; the thought of walking back—voluntarily!—into that lions' den made her feel weak inside!

Jed nodded abruptly. 'Tomorrow will do.'

'Tomorrow…?' Her eyes widened. 'But—is Grandie *that* ill?'

'Your concern is a little late in coming, but no doubt Grandie will be too pleased to see you to care too much about that!' It was obvious from his own tone that he didn't share the sentiment!

Georgie's hands clenched so tightly into fists that she could feel her fingernails biting into her palms. 'Is she?' she persisted tautly.

Jed shrugged. 'I think I'll leave you to be the judge of that for yourself.' He straightened. 'I've said all I wanted to say—'

'And that's it, is it?' Georgie attacked incredulously. 'You come here completely unexpectedly, take advantage of your host's hospitality by invading the bedroom of one of his guests. Then you tell me that Grandie is ill and wants to see me, and refuse to say anything else?' She was breathing hard by the end of her outburst, her eyes blazing, her cheeks fiery in her outrage.

'That's it exactly,' Jed answered with complete calm.

Yes, that was it, wasn't it? Jed had always said exactly what he wanted to say, and no more. And, as she knew from the past, no amount of questioning, wheedling, asking, would make him say any more if he chose not to do so.

As he chose not to now...

'Tomorrow could be a little—difficult,' she said slowly.

'What's difficult about it?' Jed replied. 'I'm sure that if you explained to the Lawsons that you have to leave in order to deal with a family problem they would understand. Or is it Andrew Lawson you're worried about?' he added shrewdly. 'Tell me, Georgie, how can you be engaged to marry a man, and yet that same man knows absolutely nothing about you that matters?' he demanded.

'All Andrew needs to know about me is that I love him!' she returned, her cheeks flushed red with anger.

'I thought I knew that you loved me once, too,' Jed shot back harshly. 'For all the good it did me!'

Georgie drew in a deeply controlling breath, knowing that to allow this conversation to—once again!—deteriorate into a slanging match would achieve nothing.

'I'll see what I can do about going to see Grandie tomorrow,' she told him evenly.

Jed's mouth thinned. 'I should try to do more than see what you can do, if I were you,' he advised.

Georgie stiffened at his tone of voice. 'Or what...?' she prompted warily.

'I wasn't aware that I had said there was an "or what",' he denied, moving towards the bedroom door.

Her chin rose defensively. 'I know from experience that there usually is where you're concerned!'

Jed turned before opening the door. 'Isn't it time you got over this childish belief that I'm some sort of monster?'

She had thought she had! Until faced with Jed once again...

She sighed, giving a self-disgusted shake of her head. 'What time is best for visiting Grandie?' That's it, Georgie, stick to the point. That way there was less chance for this verbal fencing she and Jed seemed to fall into whenever they did happen to meet—by chance or design!

'What you really mean is what time would be best not to find your grandfather at home?' Jed derided knowingly. 'Tomorrow is Saturday, Georgie; even your grandfather doesn't work at the weekend!'

'There was a time when he did,' she defended.

'He's seventy-eight years old, for goodness' sake,' Jed responded. 'Even he recognises that it's time he slowed down. Besides,' he added heavily, 'Grandie's heart attack has been a shock to him.'

Georgie could understand that. Estelle Lord, Jed's grandmother, and George Jones, Georgie's grandfather, had met and fallen in love fifteen years ago, marrying only months later. Both of them were aware that they had found this second-time-around love rather late in their lives and had been determined to enjoy together the years they had left.

Georgie knew that her grandfather would be devastated now by his wife's sudden illness.

'So, to answer your question, Georgie,' Jed continued firmly, 'in view of the fact that neither my grandmother nor your grandfather has set eyes on you in two years—any time is probably a good time to go and see them! In fact, I would say it's past time!'

Georgie's mouth tightened at the rebuke. 'You—'

'You know, Georgie, I still can't believe you did that,' Jed opined. 'You decided you no longer wanted to be married to me—fine. But to include your grandfather and Grandie in your desertion—'

'I didn't desert anyone,' she defended heatedly.

'No?' Jed raised dark brows. 'That's not the way I remember it.'

She shook her head, knowing she couldn't stand much more of this. 'Think what you like, Jed,' she said wearily. 'You usually do anyway— Forget I said that!' She winced as she instantly realised she was lapsing into childishness once again.

'Thank you for letting me know about Grandie. I'll go and see her some time tomorrow.' When she had built up her courage for the inevitable meeting with her grandfather such a visit would incur.

'Very politely put,' Jed said. 'Make sure that you do.'

'I—'

'You know, Georgie, I was wrong earlier. When I

claimed that my wife divorced me because she understood me,' he explained huskily at her puzzled expression. 'You don't understand me at all, do you? I don't think you ever did,' he added heavily. 'For instance,' he continued softly as Georgie would have spoken, 'what do you think I would like to do at this precise moment?'

'You should have made it something more difficult than that, Jed! Strangulation comes to mind,' she suggested ruefully.

He shook his head slowly. 'What I would most like to do at this moment is lie down on that bed with you and make love to you all night. But as I know that is never going to happen...'

Georgie could only stare at him as he left the bedroom as abruptly as he had first appeared in it.

She sank down gratefully onto the side of the bed, her breath leaving her in a ragged sigh of exhaustion. Had Jed been serious about that last claim? Could he really, even after all this time, want to make love with her?

She didn't know—wasn't sure of anything any more. Anything to do with Jed always left her feeling confused.

And she didn't think her meeting with her grandfather, a man almost as forceful and arrogant as Jed, was going to be any easier...!

CHAPTER FOUR

SHE didn't feel much better the following day as she hesitated outside her grandfather's Belgravia home. She was so nervous her legs were shaking and her palms felt damp. Almost as if she had never been to the house before. Which was ridiculous; she had lived here with her grandfather until she was eighteen years old. Before she married Jed...

Her resolve deepened as she thought of him. Of their marriage. Of the reason for it.

She had no reason to feel in the least nervous about this visit; if anyone should feel uncomfortable about it then it should be her grandfather!

'Miss Georgie!' the butler's pleasure in seeing her as he opened the door was unmistakable. He was an elderly man of unguessable years, although he had certainly been working for her grandfather for as long as Georgie had lived here.

Well, at least one person was pleased to see her! 'Good afternoon, Brooke.' She smiled in response to his greeting. 'I'm here to see Grandie,' she explained, less confidently; after all, there was no guarantee that her grandfather would agree to her doing that. After the way they had parted two years ago, he might not even let her inside the house!

'Of course.' Brooke stood back to allow her entrance. 'We've been expecting you,' he added warmly.

47

Georgie paused as she stepped inside, giving him a startled look. 'You have...?'

'We have,' remarked an all-too-familiar voice. Georgie turned in time to see Jed strolling into the large hallway from the family sitting room, his brows rising mockingly as he saw the surprised look on her face. 'Thanks, Brooke. I can handle things from here,' he dismissed the elderly butler.

'It's wonderful to see you again, Miss Georgie,' Brooke told her before disappearing down the stairs that led into the realms of the Victorian kitchen.

Georgie eyed Jed uncertainly. What was he doing here? He had already left the Lawson house by the time she'd gone down to breakfast late this morning, but he hadn't mentioned anything last night about being at her grandfather's house today...

'Grandie is looking forward to seeing you.' Jed broke into her thoughts. 'I have no idea how your grandfather feels about it.'

As if he had known exactly what her next question was going to be! And perhaps he did. She had never been a complicated person to understand!

Jed grinned. 'He made no comment when I told him you would be coming to see Grandie today. Nor has he made one since.'

When he had told her grandfather she *would* be coming to see Grandie today... He had been so sure, then, that she *would* come?

'Is Grandie upstairs in her bedroom?' Georgie wasn't sure how ill Estelle was, whether or not she had been moved to a ground-floor room so that she didn't have the bother of climbing the stairs.

'She is,' Jed confirmed grimly. 'Georgie, there's something I have to tell you before you see Grandie—'

'You came, then,' rasped a harshly critical voice.

Georgie turned sharply, to see her grandfather standing in the hallway that led to his private study. He was a tall, autocratic man, his hair iron-grey and his face was deeply lined but still showed signs of how handsome he had been in his youth. At the moment his deep green eyes, so like Georgie's own, were as hard as the jewels they resembled!

No forgiveness there, then. Perhaps as well, because there was no forgiveness on her part either!

She swallowed hard. 'Grandfather,' she greeted him tersely.

'Georgina,' he returned curtly. 'It's nice to see you still have enough sensitivity of feeling left to come and visit Estelle.' His voice softened with tenderness as he spoke of his beloved wife.

It was a love-match. The marriage of George Jones and Estelle Lord might have combined their two hotel chains into the forceful L & J Group, but Georgie had never doubted that George and Estelle loved each other deeply. She had come to doubt many other things about her grandfather, but never that!

Her chin rose challengingly. 'If I had known of Grandie's illness earlier I would have come before,' she confirmed.

Her grandfather gave a scornful snort. 'You could hardly be informed of anything when you chose not to tell even your own husband where you are!'

'Ex-husband,' Georgie corrected sharply.

'I'm sure you are well aware of my feelings concerning divorce, Georgina,' her grandfather countered.

Oh, yes, she was well aware of them. In other words, he refused to recognise that she and Jed were divorced!

She gave a dismissive shrug. 'Fortunately, it's unimportant what you think—'

'Shall we go up and see Estelle now?' Jed put in, shooting Georgie a warning glance as she turned to glare at him. 'She's refused to take her afternoon nap until after she's seen you,' he went on to say.

As if Georgie should have already known that!

Really, these two men had been screwing her life into knots for far too long; the quicker she got this visit to Estelle over with, the sooner she would be able to get away from both these arrogant men.

'I'm ready whenever you are,' she assured Jed as she turned abruptly away from her grandfather.

Just looking at him, remembering their closeness in the past, was enough to break her heart. Actually having to feel the force of his displeasure towards her was almost more than she could stand.

They had always been so close in the past. Even George's marriage to Estelle fifteen years ago had not broken the bond that had arisen between them after the death of Georgie's parents. Seeing her grandfather again in these awkward circumstances was almost unbearable.

Jed was glowering heavily, and Georgie was able to feel the vibrations of his displeasure as they walked up the wide staircase together.

But instead of turning left at the top of the stairs, in the direction of the bedroom Estelle shared with Georgie's grandfather, Jed turned suddenly to the right.

Georgie came to a halt. 'Where are you going?' she demanded, well aware of the bedrooms that lay in this direction.

Jed's gaze was flinty grey as he paused to look at her. 'I need to talk to you before you see Grandie,' he said seriously.

She eyed him warily. 'Why?'

'There are some things you need to—be made aware of before you see her.'

Georgie gave him an impatient glance. 'I'm not a child, Jed. I do know what illness looks like!'

'I'm sure you do, but—'

'But nothing, Jed.' She cut across him, turning determinedly in the direction of Estelle's bedroom. 'Are you coming with me or not?'

He struggled to hide his irritation with her. 'I'm coming with you,' he confirmed tersely, his hand lightly clasping the top of her arm as he walked down the hallway beside her. 'Just remember, I did try to explain the situation to you,' he said enigmatically.

Georgie gave herself a mental shake; Jed could be as mysterious as he pleased, but she refused to become embroiled in any of his games.

'I'll remember,' she assured him reluctantly.

To say that she wasn't dismayed by the changes she could see in Estelle would have been to tell a lie. The older woman had always been tiny and delicate to look at, but that delicacy had been teamed with a seemingly boundless vitality. Now Estelle merely looked frail as she sat in a chair looking out over the garden at the back of the house. There was not an ounce of superfluous flesh on her tiny frame, and her hands were almost clawlike as they rested on top of the rug that covered her legs. Her face was still beautiful, but obviously ravaged by the illness that had struck so suddenly.

But the deep lines of illness were dispelled as her face lit up with pleasure, blue eyes bright with emotion at the sight of Georgie. 'Georgie!' she breathed excitedly, holding out her hands in welcome.

'Grandie!' Georgie went to her unhesitatingly, clasping the slender hands in both of hers as she went down on her knees beside Estelle's chair. 'Oh, Grandie,' she repeated emotionally, holding the iciness of one of those waif-like hands against the warmth of her own cheek.

'Jed said he would bring you, but I— Oh, my dear, it's so good to have you back,' Estelle assured her emotionally, tears of happiness welling in her deep blue eyes.

As if Georgie needed any such assurance; the older woman's pleasure in seeing her was enough to bring tears into her own eyes. Along with a certain feeling of guilt. How could she have cut herself off so irrevocably from this lady who had shown her nothing but kindness from the moment the two of them met, who had sheltered and nurtured her as if she were the daughter Estelle had lost so long ago?

'Almost the return of the Prodigal,' Jed drawled from somewhere behind her.

Reminding Georgie all too forcefully that he was the main reason she had behaved in the way that she had the last two years. Jed. And her grandfather.

She sat back on her haunches, giving Jed a censorious glare before turning back to smile gently at Estelle. 'It's good to be back,' she said firmly.

'Mmm, pretty.' Estelle touched Georgie's hair. 'Your grandfather will be so pleased to see you!'

'Yes,' Georgie confirmed vaguely, sure that 'pleased' wasn't the best word to describe how her grandfather had looked when he had seen her a few minutes ago!

Estelle's expression became compassionate. 'He's missed you so much, Georgie,' she confided. 'We all have.' She squeezed Georgie's hand encouragingly.

Georgie deliberately didn't look at Jed after this last statement, sure that he didn't share his grandmother's feelings. 'I would have come before, Grandie, if I had known you weren't well—'

'I know you would, my dear,' Estelle accepted warmly. 'Such a silly argument, wasn't it?' she said sadly. 'But it's all over now, isn't it?' She brightened.

Georgie hesitated. Was it 'all over'…? Neither Jed nor her grandfather had given her that impression earlier…

'Now we can just get back to being a happy family again,' Estelle continued with satisfaction. 'And we were a happy family, weren't we, Georgie?'

They had been, yes. Briefly. But—

'I think we've stayed long enough for now, Grandie.' Jed was the one to excuse them gently, stepping forward to draw Georgie back onto her feet at his side, retaining that hold on Georgie's arm as they stood together looking down at Estelle. 'We'll come back after your nap,' he assured his grandmother as she would have protested.

Estelle relaxed back in her chair. 'Of course you will,' she accepted with a happy sigh. 'We have all the time in the world now, don't we?'

Georgie was alerted. 'What—?'

'Come along, darling,' Jed cut in, his hand firm on

her arm as he turned her towards the doorway. 'Grandie needs to rest now,' he insisted.

Georgie was totally bewildered by Estelle's remarks—so bewildered that she allowed herself to be determinedly guided from Estelle's bedroom, Jed's hand still tightly gripping her arm.

But only for as long as it took him to close the bedroom door behind them. Georgie instantly pulled out of his grasp. Although, no doubt, she would have bruises on her arm later to show for her bid for independence!

'Exactly what is going on?' she demanded of Jed. 'Estelle seemed under the impression—'

'Let's go somewhere less—public,' Jed replied as one of the maids passed through the lower hallway.

'But—'

'That wasn't a request, Georgie,' Jed grated between clenched teeth. 'I'm not in the habit of discussing private family matters where anyone can overhear!' he added, before striding off in the direction of the hallway opposite.

The hallway Georgie had veered away from so determinedly earlier on. The hallway where the bedroom she had once shared with Jed was situated…!

'No, Jed.' She stood her ground, her chin raised defensively as he stopped to turn and look at her with narrowed eyes.

His mouth twisted derisively. 'I want to talk to you, Georgie—not make love to you!' he announced insultingly.

'Love!' she repeated scathingly. 'I don't remember there being too much love in our relationship!' Except on her side… She had once loved Jed to distraction.

With blindness where his own motives for their marriage were concerned!

She had been so besotted with him five years ago, so much in love with him, that when he'd asked her to marry him she hadn't even noticed that there were no words of love forthcoming on his side. That realisation had come later. Much later.

Jed sighed, shaking his head impatiently. 'If this isn't the place to discuss Estelle's—condition, then it certainly isn't the place to discuss our marriage!' he snapped coldly, before resuming his progress down the carpeted hallway.

To Georgie's surprise he went straight past the doorway of the bedroom that had once been her own, and then later the bedroom the two of them shared as husband and wife, only stopping when he reached the room that he had occupied in the past whenever he'd come to stay with Estelle and George.

He turned as he opened the door. 'Satisfied?' he said.

Not exactly, but she supposed it would have to do. After all, she had no wish to discuss family matters where any of the household staff could overhear either.

His chilling grey gaze moved over her mockingly as she swept past Jed into the bedroom. 'That's the first sensible thing you've done since we met again last night!' he derided as he followed her into the room and closed the door behind him.

Georgie was far from sure about having that bedroom door closed. She felt distinctly uncomfortable in the intimacy of the room where Jed had stayed immediately after Estelle and Georgie were married and, later, on the occasions when he'd come to visit after he had moved into his own apartment at twenty-one.

On the surface of it, she and Jed had very similar backgrounds: both had been brought up by their respective grandparents from a very young age, although the necessity for Jed to live with Estelle had been vastly different from the death of Georgie's parents.

Jed's father, as far as Georgie could ascertain, had been a complete mystery—might have been any one of a number of lovers his mother had had in her life at that particular time.

His mother had been someone Estelle had even refused to have mentioned in Georgie's hearing, disgusted that her daughter could have just abandoned her baby son of four years old in order to go to live in France with yet another lover.

Jed had never talked of his mother, and because Estelle had refused to even have her name mentioned Georgie had never really got to know anything about the other woman. It had worried her a little when she and Jed were married, wondering how she was going to explain the situation to any children they might have had. But obviously *that* situation was no longer even a possibility...

Georgie shook her head, deliberately hardening her heart to the signs of Jed's earlier occupancy of the room; the worn paperback books on the bookcase beside the single bed, the masculine wallpaper and bed linen, a rugby ball he had used at university, the trophies and cups he had won for both rugby and rowing.

She looked across at Jed unflinchingly. 'Would you

like to tell me what's going on?' she demanded, refusing to rise to his deliberate insult of a few minutes ago.

'I would ask you to sit down, but as the only available space seems to be the bed...' He trailed off.

She could feel the heat that entered her cheeks even as she drew in a sharply controlling breath. Jed had been deliberately goading her, in one way or another, since the two of them met again the previous evening, and she wasn't going to give him the satisfaction of rising to those insults.

'Jed, you asked me to come here today, and at considerable awkwardness to myself I've done so, but—'

'What did you tell Lawson about that, by the way?' he interrupted her mildly. 'Not the truth, I'm sure,' he added dryly.

Her mouth firmed. 'My relationship with Andrew is none of your business—'

'The hell it isn't!' Jed responded.

Georgie's frown turned to one of puzzlement. 'Jed, we've been divorced for six months now—'

'I know exactly how long it's been, Georgie,' he returned swiftly, a nerve pulsing in his tightly clenched jaw.

'Well, then,' she muttered, no longer quite meeting his gaze.

He could have no idea of the strength it had taken to leave him in the first place, let alone actually go through with the divorce. But, having done those things, she wasn't going to back down now. And she certainly wasn't going to be fooled into thinking Jed actually cared that she had divorced him!

'Well, then,' he repeated. 'You've grown up a lot in

the last two years, Georgie,' he opined, changing the subject.

She looked up at him, eyeing him warily. 'Maybe I have,' she conceded, 'but I'm obviously still not in your league when it comes to getting my own way.' After all, no matter how she felt about it personally, she was here, wasn't she?

His mouth firmed. 'I asked you to come here for Grandie's sake, not mine,' he replied.

'Believe me, that's the only reason I came!' she assured him.

'Nice to know you still care about one member of this family,' Jed replied, with more than a hint of sarcasm.

Her eyes flashed deeply green. 'Grandie, as far as I'm aware, has never used or deceived me!'

'What the hell does that mean?' Jed exclaimed, taking a step towards her.

A step Georgie took exception to, her expression glacial now, the look in her eyes warning him not to come any closer. 'Grandie seems…under the impression that we're all friends again now…' she said slowly.

'Friends!' Jed repeated scornfully. 'Were the two of us ever friends?'

Georgie flinched, at the same time furious with herself as she felt the sting of tears behind her lids, angry with herself that this man could still manage to hurt her.

Because, yes, the two of them had been friends. Maybe that friendship had always been a little one-sided—eight-year-old Georgie following Jed about adoringly whenever he was at home, and as an infatuated teenager gazing at him in the same way as she grew older. But Jed had seemed to be kind to her then, gentle—two things she could never accuse him of being now!

'Maybe not,' she accepted dully. 'Tell me about Grandie,' she prompted abruptly.

He drew in a sharp breath. 'I told you she had a heart attack three weeks ago. Would you like to cast your mind back to what other event took place three weeks ago?' He furrowed dark brows.

Three weeks ago...? What on earth—?

Her eyes widened incredulously. 'You aren't trying to tell me that my engagement—the announcement of my engagement to Andrew—had anything to do with it?' That would just be pushing things too far! Although it was exactly three weeks yesterday since that announcement had appeared in *The Times*...

Jed's mouth thinned at her obvious scepticism. 'I'm not trying to tell you anything—because I already know it had everything to do with it!'

'But—'

'George went up to have coffee with her as usual that morning, and found her slumped over the newspaper,' Jed explained. 'He discovered later—once the doctor had come, and Grandie had been rushed to hospital— that the newspaper was open on the page containing the announcement of your engagement to Andrew Lawson!'

Georgie stared at him. He couldn't be serious? He didn't really think—? Her grandfather didn't believe—?

But she could see from Jed's accusing expression that he did think that. Not only did he think that, but he totally believed it. Which had to mean her grandfather believed it too...

But what did they want her to do about it? What *could*

she do about it? She loved Andrew. The two of them were going to be married. So what—?

Her gaze sharpened suspiciously as she remembered something. 'Grandie said something earlier about us all being a happy family again…?'

Jed agreed. 'Because that's what she thinks we are.'

'What?' Georgie stared at him, incredulous.

He gave a confirming inclination of his head. 'Grandie believes us to have reconciled our differences. That your engagement was a mistake. That the two of us are back together.'

Georgie's eyes had got wider and wider as Jed spoke. 'How on earth—? Why—? Who could have told her such a thing—? You!' she instantly guessed, staring at Jed accusingly as she recognised that challenging tightening of his jaw. 'You told Grandie—gave her the impression that the two of us— How could you?' she gasped disbelievingly. 'How *could* you?' she repeated, dazed.

'What choice did I have?' Jed returned vehemently, hands clenched into fists at his sides.

'What choice?' Georgie repeated incredulously.

'Grandie was very ill—could have died. I—I decided that if it was seeing the announcement of your engagement in the newspaper that had made her ill, then the best way to help her get better was to tell her it had all been a mistake, that the two of us were back together!'

'*You* decided?' Georgie questioned forcefully, so angry she was shaking. 'What right did you have to decide any such thing? *Who* gave you the right?' she amended furiously.

Jed's expression was icy cold now as he met her accusing gaze unflinchingly. 'My love for my grandmother gave me that right,' he told her. 'Tell me you wouldn't you have done the same thing if it had been your grandfather's life that hung in the balance,' he added hardly.

Georgie's anger left her so quickly she felt like a deflated balloon.

Would she have done what Jed had if it had meant safeguarding her grandfather's life? Would she have lied in the way he had to achieve that end?

She and her grandfather had had their differences, there was no doubting that, but— Yes, Georgie knew without a doubt that she would have done exactly what Jed had if it would have brought her grandfather back from the jaws of death!

But now that Jed *had* done it, exactly where did that leave them?

More to the point, where did that leave her and Andrew?

CHAPTER FIVE

'REMEMBER, Georgie, I did try to warn you earlier—'

'You didn't try hard enough!' she bit out fiercely, glaring across the bedroom at Jed, knowing that he *had* tried to warn her; but how could she possibly have guessed the enormity of what he was trying to tell her?

Jed thrust his hands into the pockets of his black denims, unwittingly drawing Georgie's reluctant attention to his lean muscularity, the width of his shoulders, tapered waist and the long length of his legs.

She didn't want to be here, Georgie realised with panic. Didn't want to get drawn back into this family. Certainly didn't want to get drawn back into close proximity with Jed!

'Okay, so you did try to warn me,' she conceded impatiently, unaware that she was now pacing the room.

'That's something, I suppose,' Jed accepted dryly, watching her anxious movements. 'But the real question is, do you accept the reasons why I did what I did?'

The honest answer to that was—yes, she did understand. But honesty on her part wouldn't change the unacceptable position into which Jed's lie had now put her. Or the anger she felt towards him for doing so!

She looked at him crossly. 'How well is Grandie now?'

'Not as well as she thinks she is—and certainly not as well as you would like her to be!'

Georgie stiffened at his taunt, knowing that Jed was aware of exactly how she felt about this situation. A situation she didn't intend letting continue for a moment longer than was absolutely necessary. The question was; how long was necessary...?

'The months following a first heart attack are the most dangerous,' Jed told her frankly. 'Because a second one, quickly afterwards, could prove fatal.'

How did he do that? How did he manage to read her mind now, enough to be able to answer questions before she had even asked them, when for the three years of their marriage he hadn't seemed to know how she felt about anything!

Georgie stopped her pacing to look at him hard. 'So where does that leave us? Me,' she added. Because she really wasn't interested in Jed, or the life he now led, was she?

Jed raised dark brows. 'As far as Grandie is concerned? No longer engaged to Lawson. But not yet re-married to me.'

'This is—this is intolerable!' Georgie burst out. 'You had no right, Jed. No right at all!' She resumed pacing the room, her movements those of a trapped animal.

'For goodness' sake stand still, Georgie,' Jed snapped irritably. 'You're making me dizzy!'

'I'm making you—!' She shook her head disgustedly. 'Grandie has to be told the truth, Jed,' she told him firmly. 'She has to know that—'

'And are you going to take responsibility for what comes next?' Jed cut in. 'Are you?' he pressed.

She had been shocked by the changes she had found in Estelle, deeply disturbed by the older woman's frailty.

She certainly didn't want to be the cause of further distress. But the price she would have to pay for Estelle's continuing health—having to keep up some sort of pretence of a reconciliation with Jed, in front of Estelle at least—could be her own sanity!

Besides, how could she ever explain any of this to Andrew…?

'Tell you what, Georgie.' Jed broke into her troubled thoughts. 'You do this for Grandie and I'll double the offer I've made Gerald Lawson for his land.'

'Don't be ridiculous, Jed,' she responded distractedly. 'I'm not in the least interested in your business dealings with Gerald.'

'But he is,' Jed assured her softly.

'I don't understand…' Georgie looked at him frowningly, completely puzzled by the strange turn this conversation had taken. What on earth did her future father-in-law have to do with any of this?

Jed looked grim. 'Gerald Lawson is in trouble, Georgie. Financial trouble.'

She hadn't known that—had always assumed, from the way they lived, that the Lawson family were extremely wealthy. Not that it made any difference to her if they weren't; it was Andrew she was marrying, not his family. Although it did explain that slight feeling of something being left unsaid she had experienced the evening before, when Andrew had mentioned the proposed business deal between his father and Jed.

'An injection of a few million would certainly go a long way to easing the situation,' Jed continued.

Georgie had no idea why he was persisting with this. Gerald was Andrew's father, and she felt for him, and the family, if he was in financial difficulty. But it would make no difference to her feelings for Andrew if Gerald were to lose all his money tomorrow.

'I told you,' she persisted, 'that is nothing to do with me—'

'No?' Jed challenged. 'I suppose you know that Annabelle Lawson had a nice wealthy Lady Someone-or-other picked out as the wife of her only son? Before he produced you, of course,' Jed added dryly.

'What are you talking about?' Georgie exclaimed exasperatedly, having no idea what any of this had to do with Grandie's condition.

Although, if what he said about Annabelle was true, that might explain the other woman's reticence towards her as a prospective daughter-in-law...

Jed seemed unmoved by the emotion in her voice. 'Sukie mentioned her mother's hopes concerning Andrew yesterday evening. It appears that as far as the Lawson family is concerned you're a bit of a dark horse, Georgie,' he said. 'No family of your own—or so it appears to them. A first-time author of a children's book. Not quite what Mummy was hoping for as the wife of her only son and heir!' he concluded.

Not that it was any of Jed's business, but she was already well aware of that fact. She had just hoped that, with time, when Annabelle saw that Andrew was happy with Georgie, she would come to accept her and the situation.

'I'm not marrying Andrew's mother!' she stated firmly.

'I doubt that Gerald would marry her either, given his time over again,' Jed drawled. 'She's most of the reason he's in such a financial mess,' he explained at Georgie's questioning look. 'She likes to live the life of the Lady to the full. House in London, country estate, apartment in New York, private education for both her children. The right friends. The right social gatherings.' He paused, then went on. 'And to think, when she and Gerald first met, he was just a graduate with a vague interest in politics, and Annabelle was the daughter of a postman!'

'I happen to like Gerald very much,' Georgie told him defensively.

'So do I,' Jed agreed. 'He was a good politician. Did you ever wonder why it was he retired two years ago, at only fifty?'

'No,' Georgie sighed. 'But I'm sure you're going to tell me,' she added wearily.

She still had no idea where this conversation was going, but Jed's words were hypnotic.

'He got out before the whole castle he'd built on sand came crashing down around his ears and caused a public scandal.' Jed grimaced.

'How do you know these things, Jed?' Georgie looked at him uncomprehendingly.

He shrugged. 'I made it my business to find out.'

'Why?' But she was afraid she already knew the answer to that question. Oh, not that she thought it had anything to do with Jed actually minding that she was engaged to marry someone else. He needed something from her. And he wasn't a man who liked to ask for anything...

He gave her a half-smile. 'I'm sure you've already worked that one out for yourself.'

Oh, yes, she had worked it out. But she was no nearer knowing what he expected her to do about it.

'You see, Georgie,' Jed continued evenly, 'Gerald needs either a large inflow of money to pay off the accumulation of debts, or for his son to marry a woman with money. And as the last time I spoke to your grandfather on the subject you had told him exactly what he could do with your inheritance, you don't appear to be that woman!'

Georgie *had* received a large sum of money, that had been left in trust to her by her parents, when she was twenty-one. But it was money she had used to buy her own apartment after she and Jed separated—money she had used to live on while writing her book. She had received an advance payment on her book, but any royalties would take some time to materialize. And as she was determined not to accept anything from her grandfather...!

'Andrew isn't in the least interested in money,' she said defiantly, although even she could hear a certain amount of defensiveness in her tone.

'No one is—until it's no longer there,' Jed drawled knowingly. 'Come on, Georgie, be honest; didn't you find it a little hard after you had left—once you had distanced yourself from the family? Learning to live within a budget, knowing there were certain things you could no longer afford to do?'

Yes, never having had to do that before, having first lived with her grandfather and then married Jed, it had been hard to suddenly be on her own, to manage the money her parents had left her. But there had been benefits too—and no longer being answerable to her grandfather—or Jed—had definitely been one of them! Although that situation didn't exactly apply where the Lawson family were concerned, did it...?

She shook her head dismissively. 'Andrew lives perfectly well on the salary he earns as a junior partner—'

'The rent on his apartment is paid for by his parents. His car was also bought by them. As was—'

'How do you *know* these things?' Georgie demanded; he knew more about Andrew's financial situation than she did!

'Just take it that I know, okay,' Jed replied. 'You—'

'No, I won't "take" any such thing,' she cut in accusingly. 'What does it matter about Andrew's apartment. We can both live in mine after we're married. As for his car—'

'Georgie, I think you're missing the point,' Jed interrupted softly, grey gaze enigmatic.

She glared at him frustratedly. 'That point being?'

He gave a humourless smile. 'Without that large cash inflow I spoke of earlier materialising during the next few months, Andrew Lawson's father is going to have to declare himself bankrupt.'

Georgie became very still as she looked across at him, very conscious of the way in which Jed had phrased that statement; not just that Gerald Lawson would have to declare himself bankrupt, but that *Andrew's father* would have to do so...

Because although it might not bother her whether Andrew's family were as rich and influential as they gave the impression of being—in fact, it might be easier for her if they weren't!—it would assuredly bother Andrew if his family were put in that position. And not only because he would be deeply upset to see that happen to his parents, but because it might—just might—affect his chances of rising any further in the law firm he was associated with.

A fact Jed was well aware of, if his satisfied expression was anything to go by!

She gave a disgusted shake of her head. 'If Gerald's piece of land is that valuable, then I'm sure he could find another buyer for it,' she surmised.

'Not for the inflated price the L & J Group is willing to pay for it,' Jed assured her.

Georgie looked at him intently. 'How inflated?'

'Enough to settle Gerald's outstanding debts and leave him a million or so over with which to start again.'

Georgie wasn't even going to ask how he knew all that about Gerald Lawson's private business. She knew Jed well enough to know he wouldn't be saying this at all if he weren't absolutely sure of his facts. It was his reason for bothering to find out those things that was of more interest to her...

'Would you like to get to the bottom line here, Jed?' she said slowly.

He gave a rueful grin. 'Since when did you become a "bottom line" person?'

'Since the beginning of this conversation,' she returned unhesitant.

Jed smiled widely, his eyes a deep smoky grey now. 'You know, Georgie, you're really rather beautiful in this mood,' he said appreciatively.

She sighed her impatience. 'If that's meant to be some sort of compliment, Jed—don't bother! I stopped looking for any sort of approval from you long ago.'

His expression tightened speculatively. 'Did you now?' he murmured.

'Yes! I—' Georgie's words were choked off as she found herself being pulled determinedly into Jed's arms, his face mere inches away from hers as he looked down at her. 'Let me go, Jed!' she ground out from between gritted teeth, standing absolutely rigid and unresponsive within the circle of his arms.

Not that she felt completely unresponsive inside. Part of her wanted to scream and shout at him to release her. But another part of her—the part that needed to be heard!—was burning with a remembered desire.

'And if I don't?' Jed finally returned mildly—when Georgie had got to the point when she thought she would have to scream and shout for her release after all!

She looked up at him unflinchingly. 'Then I'll be forced to stamp on your toes!'

Jed's eyes widened incredulously for a few brief seconds, then he immediately gave another smile, that quickly turned to open laughter.

Much to Georgie's amazement. Oh, not that she particularly liked the fact that he was apparently laughing at her. But to see Jed laughing at all was a complete surprise to her. It had been so long since she had seen him smile, let alone laughing like this, she realised with affection.

Finally, as his laughter ceased, Jed looked down at her, his hold having loosened about her waist, although he didn't completely release her. 'I'll have you know I'm wearing hand-made Italian shoes,' he informed her.

'In that case, in a few moments they're going to be crushed handmade Italian shoes,' Georgie told him lightly, not absolutely sure what had actually happened between them just now, but nevertheless knowing that a moment of danger had passed.

Danger…?

Yes—danger. Because she had no doubt in her mind that Jed had been about to kiss her before she made him laugh instead. And, in all honesty, she wasn't sure how she would have reacted to that kiss…

Jed stepped back, his arms falling lightly back against his sides. 'Perhaps not,' he accepted.

Georgie felt as if she could finally breathe again, although she could still feel the imprint of Jed's arms about her waist—still felt a sensitive tingling against her skin where he had touched her.

She gave a pained frown at the realisation. She had thought she was completely over Jed, that their disastrous marriage had cured her of any feelings she had for him. But that tingling of her skin just at his touch told a completely different story…

What a fool, she admonished herself inwardly. What an idiot. This man had never loved her, had married her for one reason only. And it had nothing whatsoever to do with loving her.

She drew in a harsh breath before looking across at him with hard green eyes. 'The bottom line?' she reminded him.

'Ah, yes…' he recalled, his own gaze narrowing guardedly as he straightened. 'Well, obviously, for the moment Grandie has to be kept free from stress or worry of any kind. Which is going to require a little co-operation from you—'

'Co-operation?' Georgie echoed. 'After the lies

you've told her about the two of us I think it's going to require a little more than that!'

Jed could barely conceal his irritation. 'At the time I was more interested in the immediate problem of keeping my grandmother alive than I was in any long-term repercussions that might result from those ''lies'', as you call them.'

'Well, Grandie lived—I'm happy to say,' she added before he could possibly turn any of this around on her—which she knew he was quite capable of doing, if he felt so inclined. 'But we, it seems, have been left with the problem of what to do now.'

Jed's irritation had turned to a scowl. 'I'm sure I've made myself more than plain on that subject, Georgie,' he rasped.

Maybe he had. But she just wanted to be absolutely sure before giving him her answer! 'Explain it again,' she invited mildly.

Jed's gaze narrowed suspiciously. 'I'll see that L & J Group buys Gerald Lawson's land—'

'For an inflated price,' Georgie put in.

His cheeks flushed angrily at her deliberate interruption. 'At an inflated price,' he acknowledged hardly. 'Which will give him enough cash to pay all his debts. And in return—'

'Ah, this is the part I'm most interested in,' Georgie put in with dry derision.

'In return,' Jed repeated firmly, 'I'm asking you to keep up the pretence of our reconciliation until Grandie is strong enough to be told the truth.'

That was exactly what she had thought he was saying! 'What you're actually talking about, Jed, is blackmail—of the emotional kind, if nothing else,' she said bluntly, as he would have interrupted. 'Isn't it?' she prompted as his mouth thinned angrily.

His jaw tightened and his hands clenched into fists at his sides. 'I'm talking about an exchange of—'

'Blackmail, Jed,' Georgie insisted.

His eyes flashed silvery-grey. 'All right then—blackmail,' he accepted tautly. 'What's your answer going to be?'

Georgie looked at him for several long, silent minutes, deliberately keeping her expression enigmatic; although he would have hated to admit it, Jed's uncertainty was all too easy to read from the wariness of his gaze and the tension of his body!

She knew exactly what he was asking of her, exactly what price he was willing to pay for her co-operation. And, although it might not be apparent on the surface, she was furiously angry Jed thought he needed to *buy* that co-operation!

She might have only known Grandie for fifteen years, but she loved the other woman as much as Jed did. Maybe more, in her own way, because Estelle had been the first woman in her life she could confide in.

The fact that Jed was now daring to think he could *buy* her love and loyalty to Grandie was not only hurtful, but highly insulting!

In fact, she would like nothing better at this moment than to wipe that self-confident smile right off his face! But there were more ways than one of achieving that...

Georgie gave a slight inclination of her head, her expression calm. 'Okay, Jed.'

His mouth twisted. 'My offer to help bail your fiancé's

family out of trouble proved too much of an incentive for you, hmm?'

Her expression didn't change, but her eyes hardened. 'You must do what you think right concerning that situation. I'm going back to see Grandie for a few minutes now before I leave.' She opened the bedroom door.

Jed frowned darkly. 'And that's it?' He was too stunned by her complete acquiescence to be able to hide his feelings.

'That's it,' she confirmed. 'Were you expecting a fight, Jed?' She knew well that was exactly what he had been expecting.

And how he would have enjoyed bending her to his will, forcing her to accept a situation he was sure would be completely abhorrent to her! Which was a good enough reason for her not to give him that satisfaction.

There was no disputing the fact that the situation of having to come here to spend time with Grandie would be difficult, even intolerable—and not just because of Jed. She would also have to see a certain amount of her grandfather, and she knew from her brief encounter with him earlier that neither of them had yet forgiven the other for what had happened two years ago.

But, on balance, her own satisfaction at seeing Jed completely thrown off guard by her answer was enough—for the moment!—to help her get through that awkwardness!

'Not a fight, exactly...' Jed finally responded, obviously too puzzled by her behaviour to be his usual enigmatic self.

'But you did expect to have to exert a little more pressure than you actually did?' Georgie observed. 'Perhaps maturity has taught me not to waste my energy on useless battles.' And perhaps maturity had also taught her that Jed would have preferred a battle!

Because the confused expression on his face as she quietly left the bedroom to go and see Grandie was that of a man who had not only lost *this* particular battle but also wasn't sure if he hadn't lost the war as well!

And she couldn't say it didn't give her a wonderful sense of euphoria to see Jed so disconcerted, to know that she had thoroughly confused him by her answer.

Now all she had to do was try to find some way to explain this complicated situation to Andrew...!

CHAPTER SIX

'WHEN did you cut your hair?'

Georgie, having called in to see Grandie with the promise that she would be back tomorrow, had only just congratulated herself on reaching the bottom of the wide staircase without seeing any of the rest of the family when she came to an abrupt halt, before turning to face her grandfather as he stood erect and forbidding in the doorway of the family sitting room.

Her chin rose challengingly, her expression guarded. 'About six months ago,' she answered.

'Ah.' He nodded knowingly.

Georgie met his gaze unblinkingly. 'What's that supposed to mean?'

Her grandfather shrugged broad shoulders. 'I always loved your long hair. Its colour always reminded me of the leaves of a copper beech.'

His reply didn't exactly answer her question, did it? Although she didn't really need it to, and knew exactly what he had meant.

Six months ago Georgie's divorce from Jed had become final. Three weeks later she had met Andrew at a party given by a mutual friend. But in the interim Georgie had gone to the hairdresser's and asked them to cut off the long red hair she'd had as her style since she'd been a very young child.

At first the hairdresser had protested at being asked to

despoil such natural beauty. But much to the hair-dresser's disgust, Georgie had been adamant. The result was this boyish style that framed the oval of her face. To Georgie's relief she was no longer assailed with memories every time she looked in a mirror—of the times Jed's hands had run through her hair's long copper thickness...

Strangely, Jed had made no mention of the changed length of her hair since they'd met again yesterday evening—was it really only that short a time ago? Although Grandie had commented on it a few minutes ago. And obviously her grandfather had noticed the change too!

She quirked her mouth. 'I couldn't stay eighteen for ever.'

Her grandfather gave a humourless smile. 'You were much less trouble at that age!'

Anger coloured Georgie's cheeks now. 'You—'

'Would you like to come into the sitting-room?' her grandfather invited smoothly. 'Or are we keeping you from something?' He raised iron-grey brows.

If she said no, then she would only be adding to the constraint that already existed between them. And with several weeks in front of her of having to come here, if only to see Grandie, that was not a good idea. But, by the same token, she had no wish to be ensconced in the family sitting room with her grandfather.

'Or someone...' he added.

Georgie stiffened at the implication. 'Not at all,' she replied swiftly, sweeping down the last two stairs, across the hallway, and into the sitting room.

It looked much as it had the last time she had seen it: decorated in comfortable golds and browns, the furniture old and comfortable too, well-read books and magazines on tables beside the chairs.

Strange how for Grandie and her grandfather time didn't seem to have moved on, and yet her own life had changed considerably. She was now an independent single woman, with a successful career, and a man in her life who loved her as she loved him.

And don't let any of them make you ever forget those things, Georgie, she told herself firmly, before turning to look at her grandfather once again.

'Tea?' he offered lightly.

'No, thank you.' She roused herself to refuse the offer politely.

He nodded abruptly, as if he hadn't expected her reply to be anything else. 'What did you think? Of Estelle,' he clarified curtly as she looked puzzled.

Georgie's expression relaxed; at least they were now talking of someone they both loved. 'I understand from Jed that she's been very ill——'

'I almost lost her,' her grandfather grated emotionally, his hands clenched into fists at his sides.

She had been wrong, Georgie realised, when she'd initially thought that her grandfather hadn't changed in the last two years. He looked older—lines on his face that hadn't been there before, white hair amongst the grey now too, a certain stoop to his shoulders, as if he were weighed down with the worry of the last few weeks.

Georgie felt her heart contract in her chest, knowing in that moment that no matter what had transpired between her grandfather and herself two years ago, she still loved him and cared about him—could feel his pain now, his anxiety for his wife, as if it were her own.

'I understand that, Grandfather,' she concurred. 'But Jed tells me the prognosis is good?' she continued, almost questioningly.

'As long as we can keep her happy and worry-free for a few months,' he confirmed harshly.

Jed had said a few weeks. Her grandfather now said a few months. Georgie knew which one she was inclined to believe!

'Then that's what we have to do,' she answered determinedly.

He raised grey brows. 'And your other—commitments?'

Her mouth tightened at his hesitation over that last word. But if he refused to accept her divorce from Jed, then he could hardly acknowledge her engagement to Andrew. The engagement that had precipitated Estelle's collapse...

'They don't concern you,' she dismissed, still having no idea herself how she was going to deal with this situation as far as Andrew was concerned.

The truth would be the best option, she knew, but after the way she and Jed had behaved towards each other the evening before, as if they were complete strangers, that truth could prove a little awkward to put into practice!

'In the same way that your walking out on Jed, dragging the family name through the divorce courts after effectively having abandoned that family, didn't concern me?' her grandfather returned accusingly.

Georgie stiffened at the rebuke. 'I'm willing to come here in order to help Grandie, Grandfather,' she told him sharply. 'But don't presume to think those visits will give you any rights concerning comment on my private life!' Her eyes flashed a warning.

He drew in a sharp breath. 'Your manners certainly haven't improved in the last two years,' he bit out reprovingly.

Once upon a time such a reproof from her grandfather, given in that flinty tone of voice, would have absolutely devastated her. But not any more!

She straightened, facing him squarely. 'I'll call you concerning the convenience of time for my visits to Grandie—'

'Those visits won't be in the least convincing to Estelle if you aren't accompanied by Jed.' Her grandfather cut across her words.

'I totally disagree.' She gave a derisive snort. 'Jed and I rarely did anything together even when we were married!'

'And whose fault was that?' her grandfather came back.

'Not mine,' Georgie returned without hesitation, then instantly regretted her outburst; after all this time, raking up what had or hadn't gone wrong with her marriage to Jed wasn't going to achieve anything. 'Look, Grandfather,' she reasoned heavily, 'this situation is difficult enough as it is, without the two of us continuing with the feud that exists between us. For Grandie's sake, I suggest we put all that to one side for the moment. Agreed?'

Always a dominant man, a man who liked to have the last word in most arguments, he didn't look at all happy with this suggestion. But at the same time he knew that this time he had little choice in the matter...

Finally he subsided. 'Agreed,' he bit out tautly.

Georgie let out a relieved breath—not realising until that moment that she had been holding it in!

But this really was an intolerable situation. For all of them, she was sure. The only saving grace for any of them that Georgie could see—for Jed, her grandfather, and for her—was that they were all willing to put aside their differences for the benefit of Grandie's full recovery. In front of Grandie, at least!

How the three of them really felt towards each other wasn't relevant at this point in time, and the sooner they all accepted that, the better!

'And do you think Jed will be willing to agree to the same arrangement?' her grandfather prompted harshly.

'I—'

'I think what your grandfather really means is now that you've managed to batter him into submission, perhaps you would like to start on me?' taunted an all-too-familiar voice from close behind her.

Georgie turned quickly to face Jed as he stood in the now open doorway, realizing that she and her grandfather must have been so intent on their own conversation that they hadn't been aware of Jed entering the room. At least, Georgie hadn't been aware...

She glanced back at her grandfather, knowing by the tightness about his lips that he hadn't been so innocent of Jed's presence!

Her expression was derisive as she turned back to Jed, knowing by the challenging way he returned that stare that whatever confusion he had felt earlier, over her acquiescence, he was completely over it now. 'I wouldn't even attempt to try,' she scorned. 'I've told Grandie that I will be back to see her in the morning; I leave it up to you whether or not you will be here too.'

'Oh, I'll be here,' he responded lazily. 'Didn't I tell you? I moved back in for a while when Grandie came out of hospital.'

He knew damn well he hadn't told her that! If he had, she might have been less agreeable concerning her visits here. A fact Jed was obviously well aware of!

'That's nice,' she returned with sugary insincerity. 'Well, if you gentlemen will both excuse me?' she added pointedly before turning to leave. Only to find the doorway still blocked by Jed. She met his gaze fearlessly.

Jed met that gaze for several long, silent seconds before giving a curt nod of his head and stepping to one side. 'I'll walk to the door with you,' he murmured.

Georgie gave him a scathing glance. 'I haven't forgotten the way!'

His mouth tightened. 'I'm well aware of that.'

But he obviously still had something to say to her. Something he had no intention of saying in front of her grandfather.

Georgie shrugged before preceding him from the room. If he thought—

'Thank you, Georgina.'

She came to an abrupt halt at the husky sound of her grandfather's voice, drawing in a controlling breath before she had to turn back and face him.

It had taken much more courage than she'd realised to come here at all today—she felt a little as Daniel must have done as he stepped into the lions' den!—and now all she wanted was to get away from here. Fast!

She swallowed hard, closing her eyes briefly before glancing back at him. 'You're welcome,' she muttered abruptly, giving him no opportunity to say anything further as she strode determinedly down the hallway to the front door.

She was very aware of Jed walking behind her—was also aware that he definitely wanted to say...something. She only hoped it wasn't going to be something that provoked further argument between them—because after the fraught emotion of the last hour she didn't have a lot left in reserve to get her through another verbal battle with Jed!

'Do you have your car with you, or would you like me to call a taxi?' Jed offered as she stepped out of the house into the welcome sunshine.

'It's such a nice day, I think I'll walk for a while,' she refused, breathing in the heady freedom of being outside. Away from the domineering presence of her grandfather. Away from the physical proof of Grandie's frailty. But, most of all, in a few seconds she would be free of Jed's overpowering presence too!

Once he had said whatever it was he felt he had to say to her!

He paused while he looked down at her with intense grey eyes.

Georgie waited. And waited. But still Jed just continued to look at her in that broodingly intense way.

She moved the strap of her bag more securely on her shoulder. 'I'll be back tomorrow morning, then,' she said impatiently; she didn't have all day to stand here playing guessing games with Jed!

'I…' Jed paused, breathing heavily. 'I just wanted to say thank you too,' he finally said tersely.

Georgie's brows arched in surprise, her eyes wide. This had been the last thing she had been expecting. And, oh, how it hurt Jed to be put in a position where he had to thank her!

She gave a small smile in acknowledgement of the effort it must have cost him to show her this gratitude. 'As I told Grandfather, you're welcome,' she replied.

Jed hadn't finished. 'I realise that it's Grandie you're doing this for, that given the choice you would spit in our eyes,' he acknowledged gruffly. 'But I thank you anyway.'

He wasn't wrong about spitting in their eyes, but by the same token Georgie knew both these men well—knew that it hadn't been easy for either of them to unbend enough to thank her in the way they had.

'Don't mention it,' she responded. 'Just continue to take good care of Grandie.'

'We will. And about Lawson—'

'I told you,' she put in sharply, 'I will deal with that in my own way—'

'I was referring to Gerald Lawson, Georgie,' Jed came back. 'I accept that how you explain all this to Andrew Lawson is your own affair.'

Well, that was something, at least!

'But I want you to know that I will keep my word as regards the proposed business deal with Gerald Lawson,' Jed continued.

'I never doubted it for a moment.'

'No?' Jed seemed surprised. 'You didn't seem to have the same faith in my ability to keep the marriage vows I made to you five years ago!'

Georgie felt the colour drain from her cheeks. Her lips felt suddenly numb too, and her hands clenched so tightly into fists she could feel her nails digging into her palms. But she felt glad of the slight pain that caused— it helped to override the sudden tightness she could now feel in her chest!

'Georgie—'

'Don't touch me!' she cried as Jed tried to clasp her arm, giving him a pained look and shaking her head wordlessly before turning away and hurrying down the steps that led away from the house.

How could he talk about that now? How dared he remind her—?

Because he was Jed Lord, came the instant answer. A man who felt love for no one—with the obvious, understandable exception of his grandmother. A man who could step so uncaringly over other people's emotions. A man who—

'Georgie…!' Jed groaned her name this time, having followed her in her flight from the house, his hand light on her arm as he gently turned her to face him, clasping both her arms now. 'Georgie, I can't bear to see you like this—'

'I believe I told you not to touch me!' she bit out icily, stiff with resentment as she looked coldly up into his face. '*You* can't bear it, Jed?' she spat out. 'But you're the invincible Jeremiah Lord—you can bear anything!' she derided scathingly. 'You've certainly never had a problem with hurting me in the past—and I doubt you will have any problem with it in the future either. Now, if you wouldn't mind releasing me, the middle of a busy street is hardly the time or place for this sort of conversation. In fact, I can't think of *any* time or place I want to have this conversation with you ever again. Is that clear enough for you?'

His hands had dropped away from her arms as she spoke, his expression once again blandly enigmatic. 'Very clear,' he acknowledged tightly.

'Good,' Georgie said, the colour back in her cheeks now, even if it was due to anger. 'Not the same little Georgie you remember, am I, Jed?'

Jed continued to look at her for long, timeless seconds. 'No,' he finally conceded. 'But, personally, I preferred the old Georgie,' he added at her triumphant look.

She gave a humourless smile. 'I'm sure you did. As my grandfather has already pointed out once today, I was much less trouble when I was eighteen. For ''less trouble'', read ''more gullible'',' she finished disgustedly.

Jed gave a shrug of his shoulders, his expression quizzical. 'I don't think you're going to believe me, no matter what I say in answer to that accusation.'

'I'm not going to believe anything you say to me ever again—period,' she assured him. 'Goodbye, Jed,' she said firmly, before turning on her heel and walking away—sure that, after the things she had just said, this time he wouldn't follow her.

Her step was light and determined; she was so relieved that, outwardly at least, she had managed to suppress the emotional pain the conversation with Jed had once again brought to the surface.

But, inwardly, she knew it was another matter entirely...

CHAPTER SEVEN

'BUT I don't understand, Georgie.' Andrew frowned his puzzlement.

She gave him a reassuring smile. 'It's quite simple, Andrew. As you know, I had to come back to town this morning because I learnt my grandmother is ill. Now I need to spend some time with her. That's all there is to it.'

All there was to it! She had thought long and hard about what to tell Andrew about the next few weeks, and finally decided that a simple—if not exactly complete!—explanation would do. Except Andrew looked thoroughly confused by that explanation!

Andrew had insisted on driving her back to town this morning, after she'd told him she had received a telephone call on her mobile concerning her grandmother's illness. She'd hated telling a lie about the phone call, but she could hardly tell Andrew that she knew about her grandmother's illness because Jed Lord had paid a visit to her bedroom the night before and told her about it!

Andrew had driven her home this morning so that she could drop off her things before going on to visit her grandmother. But the two of them had arranged to meet up at a restaurant for a meal together that evening. Georgie had waited until the end of their meal to break the news to Andrew about her proposed visits—alone—to her grandmother…

He shook his head now. 'That isn't what I don't understand. For one thing, I thought you told me you were brought up by your grandfather…?'

'I was,' Georgie confirmed. 'Grandie is—well, she's my grandmother on my—er—' She could hardly say on her husband's side! 'She's married to my grandfather,' she concluded.

'I should hope so.' Andrew gave a teasing smile.

Georgie looked at him ruefully. He really was the most uncomplicated of men. So kind, so warm, so—so trusting. But why shouldn't he be? Andrew couldn't possibly guess at the complication that was her family. Or the fact that she wasn't being exactly truthful about it.

'No, I mean Estelle married my grandfather when I was eight.' And brought with her the man who was to become Georgie's torment! 'But I really am very fond of her—have always thought of her as my grandmother too—as my grandmother,' she amended desperately.

Too! For there to be a 'too' there would have to be another grandchild, and Georgie had no intention of telling Andrew that the man he had met the previous evening, Jed Lord, was he.

'I see.' Andrew nodded, obviously not registering that slight slip-up on Georgie's part. 'But the other thing I don't understand is why I can't come with you on these visits…'

She shook her head. 'I told you, Grandie really has been very ill. She isn't up to seeing—strangers just yet.'

Andrew reached out and clasped Georgie's hand as it lay on the table, his fingers absently stroking her engagement ring. 'But the two of us are going to be married, so I would only be a stranger to her for the very first visit,' he reminded her.

George gave a reassuring smile. 'I appreciate that. But if I could just have your understanding for a few weeks, until Grandie is a little stronger...' She grimaced. 'I realise it's asking a lot of you, Andrew—'

'Not at all,' he hastened to reassure her. 'I'm just a little disappointed that I won't be able to see as much of you over the next few weeks. Do you realise we've seen each other every day since we became engaged three weeks ago?'

Yes, she did realise that. And those three weeks, and the previous four months when she and Andrew had been dating each other, had been absolutely wonderful.

If a little artificial...?

Much as she hated to admit it, perhaps that was so. It had been all too easy to block out the past, her family, her marriage to Jed—made life so much less complicated if she didn't have to think of those things. But it wasn't the full picture, was it? The past existed, as did her family, and sooner or later she was going to have to tell Andrew that she had once been married to Jed Lord.

But just not now...!

Andrew was looking at her so concernedly, love shining brightly for her in his trusting blue eyes; she simply couldn't bear, after the awful time she had already had, to face the possibility of losing that unconditional love and trust.

'I do know, Andrew.' She squeezed his hand. 'And I shall miss not seeing you every day too. But it will only be for a short time. And there are telephones, you know.'

She knew she was probably going to need those telephone calls as much as Andrew!

It was going to be a very difficult few weeks anyway, trying to juggle those visits to her grandfather's house—where Jed was in residence too!—so that they didn't in any way clash with her dates with Andrew, or put any sort of strain on their relationship.

'I can see that you've already made your mind up about this.' Andrew gave a resigned sigh. 'Never mind. I'm sure that we'll survive. They do say absence makes the heart grow fonder.'

'Or alternatively, out of sight, out of mind,' Georgie reminded him. 'Strange how there's always a negative response to those old-fashioned adages.'

Andrew's hand tightened on hers. 'You're never out of my mind, Georgie,' he assured her.

'I'm glad.' She squeezed his hand in return. She knew that the next few weeks were going to be difficult for her; it would certainly help to know that Andrew was waiting for her at the end of them.

Andrew sat back as the waiter delivered coffee to their table, waiting until the other man had left before resuming their conversation. 'I have a feeling I'm going to be kept pretty busy myself over the next few weeks anyway.' He grinned. 'I had a telephone call from my father this afternoon, asking me to draw up some legal papers for him. Apparently the socialising angle works; Jed Lord has offered my father an absolutely unbelievable price for that piece of land I told you about yesterday.'

Jed hadn't wasted any time in making that offer!

Or maybe he was just sewing up that particular deal to make sure she didn't go back on their agreement...?

Not that she would. But, knowing Jed, he wasn't going to take any chances.

'I hope your father grabbed the offer with both hands!'

'Yes. And no,' Andrew added consideringly. 'Oh, I'm going to draw up the required legal documents, of course, but in the meantime my father is going to check into why Lord should be making such a large offer for a piece of land valued at only half that price.'

Why hadn't either she or Jed thought about that possibility?

Or perhaps Jed had...?

It wasn't like Jed to make mistakes, especially when it came to business; surely he would have known that Gerald Lawson would become suspicious if Jed appeared too eager to finalise the deal or offered too large a sum for the land? Of course he would have known.

Her mouth tightened. 'You think this Jed Lord is up to something?'

Andrew shrugged. 'Perhaps he knows something about that piece of land that we don't.'

'Such as?' Georgie probed.

'Maybe he knows that someone else is interested in it and he intends getting his offer in first. Or maybe the government has plans for the land and would make a good offer for it.' He laughed. 'I'm not a businessman; I really wouldn't know. But when I met Jed Lord last night he certainly didn't come over as a fool to me. So if he's willing to offer a lot of money for a relatively small piece of land that was actually valued as being worth half that amount, then there has to be something about it that we don't know.'

How shocked Andrew would be if she were to tell him that what he didn't know was that she had once been Jed Lord's wife, and that was the reason for the inflated offer on the land.

But of course she intended telling him no such thing!

'Oh, well, I'm really pleased for your father.' She busied herself picking up her evening bag so that she didn't have to look at Andrew and so risk his seeing the expression of guilt she was sure was on her face. 'Shall we go?' she suggested brightly.

Damn Jed, she brooded as Andrew drove them both back to her apartment. How could he have been so stupid as to arouse Gerald's suspicions by coming back to the other man so quickly with an offer that seemed totally out of line with the current property market? Although, like Andrew, she was inclined to think the move hadn't been a stupid one on Jed's part at all. But for different reasons...

Something she intended bringing up with Jed the next time she saw him!

'You had better come through to the sitting room.' Jed sighed wearily, having taken one look at her face after Brooke had opened the door to her ring. 'Although I should warn you I don't have a lot of time, if you expect me to accompany you up to Grandie's room. I expected you earlier than this.' He glanced pointedly at the gold watch on his wrist. The hands pointed to exactly midday. 'I have an appointment at one o'clock.'

Georgie arched derisive auburn brows. 'An appointment? At one o'clock on a Sunday?' she scorned sceptically, knowing that the 'appointment' was probably with a female—and, from the casual way Jed was dressed, in black denims and an open-necked grey shirt, it had nothing to do with business. 'And I don't expect you to do anything, Jed. Grandfather was the one who thought we ought to be together when I visit Estelle,' she pointed out. 'Personally, I would rather be with anyone else other than you!' She was still smarting from the necessity of keeping these visits separate from her life with Andrew for these few weeks.

Jed scowled darkly. 'And instead you're stuck with me!'

'Not for long,' she returned forcefully.

'Surely that depends on how long it takes Grandie to make a full recovery?'

'We'll have to see, won't we?' Georgie replied uncooperatively.

Jed sighed his impatience. 'You obviously have something on your mind, Georgie, so what is it?'

'Andrew told me last night that you've made his father an offer for the land—'

'Isn't that what you wanted me to do?' Jed interrupted exasperatedly.

Georgie's eyes narrowed. 'Not so promptly that it instantly aroused suspicion, no,' she answered slowly, watching him closely to see what his reaction was to this accusation. Being Jed, a man who closely guarded his response to most things, there wasn't any visible this time either.

'And has it aroused suspicion?'

'Of course it has,' she snapped. 'Gerald wants to know why you offered so much.'

Jed shook his head exasperatedly. 'Is there *any* pleasing you, Georgie?'

'The last six months of not seeing you have been extremely pleasant,' she assured him sweetly.

'Ha-ha,' he rasped harshly. 'Shall we go up and see Grandie now?' he suggested impatiently.

'Of course,' she taunted as she swept past him out of the room. 'You mustn't be late for your date, must you?'

Jed's hand snaked out to clasp her arm tightly, halting her in her tracks. 'And what if it *is* a date I'm going on?' He glowered down at her.

Georgie shrugged. 'Then it's of absolutely no interest to me—'

'Exactly.' He nodded his satisfaction with her answer, abruptly releasing her as they walked up the wide staircase together.

Exactly.

Except...

Except for some reason she couldn't—or wouldn't—explain, Georgie found that it *was* of interest to her that Jed was going off in a few minutes to meet some mystery woman. It shouldn't be, she acknowledged with a frown, but somehow it was.

'Okay, tell me what you want me to do about Lawson,' Jed demanded, having seen her frown—and completely misunderstood the reason for it.

Thank goodness! How awful if he were to realise she was feeling some belated—and totally unacceptable!—jealousy concerning the woman he was meeting for lunch.

But perhaps this feeling was a normal response to someone you had once been married to? After all, divorce didn't automatically cut off all the feelings once felt for an ex-partner. Even Jed had acted slightly green-eyed when he saw Andrew's ring on her finger on Friday evening—and he certainly didn't love her!

She shook her head. 'I don't see that there's anything you can do now. But I'm not at all happy with the thought of Gerald snooping around to see if there's a particular reason for your over-generous offer.'

Jed grimaced. 'You think he may eventually come across the fact that my ex-wife is about to become his daughter-in-law? In those circumstances, surely I would be more inclined to let him sink in his own debts?'

That might be one reaction—if Jed had ever loved her. Which he hadn't.

'You still haven't told Andrew Lawson the truth about me, have you?' Jed realised slowly.

Guilty colour darkened her cheeks even as she avoided meeting the directness of his gaze. 'Not yet, no,' she confirmed reluctantly.

Jed snorted derisively. 'I'm the last person to be advising you about anything—'

'You most certainly are!' she replied disgustedly.

'—concerning your behaviour towards Lawson,' Jed finished decisively. 'But surely you realise, Georgie, that you're just digging a bigger and bigger hole for yourself to fall into as regards your lack of honesty towards your fiancé.' His mouth tightened over the latter word.

Her eyes widened accusingly. 'You're the last person to be lecturing me about honesty, Jed!'

He gave an impatient shrug. 'Well, don't say I didn't try to warn you...'

'Let's just go and see Grandie, hmm?' she prompted,

knocking sharply on the bedroom door and entering at Grandie's call of welcome.

Her grandmother looked a little brighter today. There was colour in her paper-thin cheeks, blue eyes sparkling with pleasure as she watched Georgie cross the room to join her in the bay window.

Georgie's own smile wavered a little at the older woman's opening remark!

'What mischief have you two been up to?' Grandie teased. 'You're both looking terribly guilty,' she added.

'Really, Grandie.' Jed moved forward to kiss his grandmother on the cheek. 'You make Georgie and I sound like naughty children!' he admonished affectionately.

Which was just as well—because Georgie had been rendered completely speechless by Estelle's reference to them looking 'terribly guilty'!

Estelle laughed softly. 'Probably because to me that's what you'll always be! Pour the tea, would you, Georgie?' she suggested lightly, indicating a tray of tea things set on the table in front of the window. 'Actually, I was wondering if the two of you had perhaps been discussing a date for your wedding?'

Georgie considered it was just as well that no one was actually looking at her at that moment—because the milk she had been pouring into the three cups ended up on the tray instead, so great was her shock at Estelle's question!

Wedding? What wedding? Okay, so Grandie considered that Georgie and Jed were once again a couple, but surely that was no reason for her to suppose—

'We don't intend rushing things this time around,

Live the emotion™
Anytime. Anywhere.
send for your 2 FREE ROMANCE BOOKS!
See Details Inside...

The Romance & Presents Collection...

We'd like to introduce you to the Romance-Presents collection, a wonderful combination of Harlequin Romance® and Harlequin Presents® books.

Your 2 FREE BOOKS will include 1 book from each series in the collection:

HARLEQUIN ROMANCE®:
Tender love stories— the essence of heartwarming romance.

HARLEQUIN PRESENTS®:
These stories are intense, international and passionate.

Your 2 FREE BOOKS have a combined cover price of over $8.00 in the U.S. and over $9.00 in Canada, but they're yours FREE!

GET A *Free* MYSTERY GIFT...

We can't tell you what it is...but we're sure you'll like it! A FREE gift just for giving the Harlequin Reader Service® Program a try!

Visit us online at
www.eHarlequin.com

Your FREE Gifts include:

- 1 Harlequin Romance® book!
- 1 Harlequin Presents® book!
- An exciting mystery gift!

HARLEQUIN®
Live the emotion™

Scratch off
the silver area to see what the
Harlequin Reader Service®
Program has for you.

YES! I have scratched off the silver area above. Please send me the **2 FREE BOOKS** and gift for which I qualify. I understand I am under no obligation to purchase any books, as explained on the back and on the opposite page.

346 HDL DU35   126 HDL DU4M

FIRST NAME	LAST NAME

ADDRESS

APT.#	CITY

STATE/PROV.	ZIP/POSTAL CODE

(H-RP-07/03)

THE HARLEQUIN READER SERVICE® PROGRAM—Here's how it work

Accepting your 2 free books and gift places you under no obligation to buy anything. You may keep the books and gift and return the shipping statement marked "cancel." If you do not cancel, about a month later we'll send you 6 additional books from the Romance-Presents collection, which includes 3 Harlequin Romance books and 3 Harlequin Presents books, and bill you just $20.73 in the U.S., or $24.12 in Canada, plus 25¢ shipping and handling per book. That's a total saving of 15% off the cover price! You may cancel at any time, but if you choo to continue, every month we'll send you 6 more books from the Romance-Presents collection, which you may either purchase at the discount price or return to us and cancel your subscription.

*Terms and prices subject to change without notice. Sales tax applicable in N.Y. Canadian residents will be charged applicable provincial taxes and GST.

Grandie.' Jed was the one to answer smoothly. 'I think Georgie deserves to be courted a little first,' he added huskily, his hand running familiarly down Georgie's spine as he did so.

So familiarly that, to Georgie's dismay, her back arched in instinctive response!

Her inner response to Jed's touch was no less disturbing, if less discernible to anyone but herself. Pleasure coursed through her body, there was a sudden tightness in her chest, and her back seemed to burn where his fingers had so lightly touched.

'What an absolutely wonderful idea, Jed!' His grandmother smiled her approval of this plan. 'We women like a little romancing, don't we, Georgie?' she said conspiratorially.

Not with Jed, Georgie didn't!

Although it would certainly be novel. The first time around, as Jed had put it, he had simply proposed to her on her eighteenth birthday. A proposal she had eagerly accepted, she recalled now with an inner cringe of embarrassment.

After the announcement of their engagement to their respective grandparents the wedding plans had moved along so fast, leaving them so little time for themselves, that before Georgie had known where she was, she was a married woman. Married to a man she had been able to realise even then, she barely knew.

Oh, she had known Jed as Estelle's loving but reserved grandson—known him as the respectful young man he always was to her grandfather. But the teasingly off-hand man she had come to know during the latter part of her own childhood had no longer been there, and in his place had been someone she couldn't relate to at all—a remote stranger. A man who was her husband.

Not a very auspicious beginning to any marriage!

Although they might even have surmounted that difficulty if Jed had been willing to bend a little, to be the lovingly attentive husband she had hoped he would be. But how could he have been? When he didn't love her at all, let alone wish to be attentive to her!

She put down the milk jug—before she managed to do any more damage with it! 'We do.' She was noncommittal in her agreement with Estelle concerning romance; she wasn't sure Jed even knew what the word meant!

Estelle eyed Jed's casually smart appearance. 'I hope he's taking you somewhere nice for lunch today, Georgie?' she teased.

He wasn't taking her anywhere!

She flickered an uncertain glance in Jed's direction. 'Er—'

'I have a business meeting lunchtime today, Grandie.' Jed was the one to answer lightly. 'So that I can free some time later in the week to spend with Georgie,' he added as his grandmother began to look upset.

So glib. So smooth. So untrue!

'Anyway, Grandie.' She turned back to the older woman, reaching out to lightly clasp Estelle's hand in her own. 'I thought I would have lunch with *you* today.' She smiled reassuringly.

'Well, of course that will be lovely, dear.' Estelle still seemed a little troubled. 'I just don't want your grandfather and I to intrude on the time you and Jed should be spending together.' She hesitated, then went on, 'I'm sure that was part of the problem last time you were together.'

Georgie was equally as sure it had nothing to do with the breakdown of her marriage to Jed!

Oh, the circumstances of their upbringing, of their respective grandparents being married to each other, had meant they were probably a much closer family unit of four than they would otherwise have been. But none of that would have mattered if Jed had loved her. If her grandfather hadn't deceived her!

'Not at all, Grandie,' Georgie assured the old lady with complete honesty, turning her attention back to pouring the tea. 'As Jed says, we can spend some time alone together later in the week.' And the moon was made of cheese!

Because her wanting to spend any time alone with Jed—ever!—was as much a fairy tale as that was!

'Of course we can,' Jed agreed, casually reaching out to rest his hand familiarly on Georgie's thigh.

Almost causing Georgie to pour the hot tea all over the tray this time!

'Would you like me to do that?' Jed offered dryly, dark brows raised mockingly as he looked pointedly at her shaking hand.

Georgie straightened resentfully, her fingers closing determinedly about the handle of the teapot. 'I can manage, thank you,' she snapped dismissively.

'Thank you, dear.' Estelle accepted the cup of tea Georgie had carefully poured for her. 'You may as well pour the fourth cup; your grandfather should be joining us in a moment.' She smiled warmly at the thought of her husband.

Georgie instinctively poured tea into that fourth cup, adding a dash of milk only, no sugar at all.

How familiar she was with those little everyday things about her grandfather, such as how he liked his tea. How he liked to read the newspaper over breakfast. How he liked a single glass of malt whisky when he came in from work in the evening. The food he preferred. The authors he read.

Yes, she knew all those small things about her grandfather—and yet two years ago she had realised in other ways she didn't really know him at all.

Jed gave a brief glance at his wristwatch before standing up. 'I'm afraid I have to go, Grandie,' he excused himself. 'Walk downstairs with me, Georgie?' he asked.

She had no inclination to go anywhere with him, especially as he was leaving her to the lions while he obviously went off with the latest woman he was involved with. But by the same token she realised that if she didn't go downstairs with him Jed was more than capable of just kissing her goodbye in front of his grandmother!

'Of course.' She stood up gracefully, although her composure deserted her a little as the bedroom door suddenly opened. Her grandfather stood in the doorway.

He raised iron-grey brows. 'Not leaving us already, are you, Georgina?' he observed disapprovingly.

Her cheeks coloured resentfully. 'I—'

'I'm the one that's leaving, I'm afraid, George.' Jed was the one to confess, stepping forward, his arm moving lightly about Georgie's shoulders as he looked across at the older man. 'I have an appointment I can't avoid.' He gave a rueful shrug. 'Georgie was just walking me down to my car,' he explained as the two of them left the room.

Georgie began to breathe a little easier once they were safely away from her grandfather, though she was not at all sure she was going to be able to cope with this. She had thought Jed was going to be her main problem during these visits to Estelle, but it was the confrontations with her grandfather that were proving the most difficult.

'He loves you very much, you know.' Jed cut softly into her worried thoughts.

Georgie gave him a withering glance as they walked outside. 'Then my grandfather's idea of love and mine are vastly different!'

Jed looked surprised. 'Somehow I doubt that.'

She had no intention of discussing the past with Jed— of all people, he was the one who should know exactly what her grandfather was capable of!

'Look—' Jed turned to her '—I accept that things didn't work out between the two of us, Georgie, but that doesn't mean—'

'That has to be the understatement of the year!' she scorned.

'You know, Georgie, bitterness is an extremely destructive emotion—'

'I'll thank you not to tell me what emotions are or aren't destructive—' Georgie's angry tirade came to an abrupt end as Jed reached out for her, his mouth coming down forcefully on hers.

And remaining there...

The force of Georgie's anger instantly melted, and the heat that now flowed through her veins, into every particle of her body, had nothing whatsoever to do with anger.

Jed's arms about her were warm and compelling, his mouth against hers firm and searching, the hardness of his body fierce and demanding.

Georgie was melting in that demand…!

It was as if the last two years had never been, as if she and Jed had never been apart, as if she still loved him—

She wrenched her mouth away from his. 'No!' she cried protestingly, desperately pushing him away from her, wanting to put as much distance between them as she possibly could. 'No,' she repeated vehemently, and Jed reluctantly released her to step back and look down at her searchingly. Two spots of colour were angry in the otherwise paleness of her cheeks, green eyes blazing with anger.

'Why did you do that?' she demanded coldly.

'Why not?' Jed returned, although his own face was slightly paler than usual, and a nerve pulsed in the rigidity of his tightly clenched jaw.

Why not—? 'If you ever touch me like that again, Jed, I'll—'

'You'll what?' he prompted quietly.

Her eyes flashed deeply green. 'I'll hit you with the first available object,' she assured him, glancing pointedly at one of the large plant pots that edged the driveway.

'Ouch!' Jed easily saw the direction of her gaze, his mouth quirking. 'That seems a little ungrateful on your part, when I was only trying to perpetuate the myth that the two of us are back together.'

Georgie looked perplexed. 'In what way could kissing me do that?'

Dark brows rose over mocking grey eyes. 'Someone in the house may be watching us out of the window—'

'Don't be ridiculous, Jed; I'm sure the staff are far too busy preparing lunch to bother spying on us!' she retorted.

'I was referring to my grandmother,' he replied evenly.

'Oh. Of course!' Georgie exclaimed, suddenly knowing that of course Jed hadn't really wanted to kiss her! 'I'm sorry if I—if I misunderstood your motives,' she added awkwardly, hating having to make the apology at all.

'Don't give it another thought,' Jed responded, a smile playing around the hard mockery of his lips as he obviously enjoyed her discomfort. 'Any message you want me to pass on to Sukie over lunch?' he enquired, even as he pressed the button on his keys to unlock his Jaguar and prepared to slide agilely inside.

Georgie's eyes widened, incredulous. Sukie—? Sukie *Lawson*? Andrew's sister? Jed's luncheon appointment was with Andrew's sister, Sukie?

'No?' Jed taunted her obvious speechlessness. 'I'll see you later, then,' he said, closing the car door with a slam.

Georgie stood dazedly in the driveway as he started up the Jaguar's engine, lowering a window to wave a hand at her as he drove away.

Jed was having lunch with Sukie Lawson!

The predatory Sukie. The cynical Sukie. The fun-loving Sukie. The beautiful Sukie...!

Georgie gave a groan, knowing that her emotional response to the thought of Jed going out with Sukie was too raw for her to mistake it for anything other than what it was.

Jealousy.

Complete and utter jealousy!

CHAPTER EIGHT

SOMETHING else occurred to Georgie as she slowly made her way back up the stairs. Estelle's bedroom was at the back of the house...

Which meant there was no possible way that Jed's grandmother could have been a witness to that affectionate parting he had claimed was for Grandie's benefit!

Georgie just didn't understand any of it. Not Jed's reason for kissing her. Not her response to it. Certainly not the jealousy she felt at knowing Jed was having lunch with Sukie Lawson!

To feel jealousy over Jed's date with another woman surely she would also have to feel love? And she certainly no longer loved Jed!

Then why had she allowed him to kiss her earlier? Worse—she had responded to it!

Well, it certainly wasn't because she loved him, she affirmed decidedly. Any love she had once felt towards Jed had been well and truly killed two years ago.

How could it not have been, after the things she had learnt about him...?

She remembered that Jed had been away on one of his frequent lengthy business trips, to the L & J Hotel in Hawaii that time. She had gone to stay with her grandfather and Estelle for a few days, to alleviate some of the boredom of being in their apartment on her own.

She had been absolutely stunned when she'd opened

the daily newspaper over breakfast and seen a photograph of Jed in the gossip pages, standing next to the beautiful blonde actress Mia Douglas.

'What is it, Georgina?' Her grandfather had leaned concernedly across the table when he saw the distress she hadn't been quick enough to hide from his astute gaze.

Georgie silently handed him the newspaper, feeling as if she had just had all the breath knocked out of her body. Jed and the actress Mia Douglas?

It couldn't be. Jed had telephoned her only the previous afternoon. Admittedly it had only been a brief conversation, but he had made no mention then of being in Los Angeles. Georgie had assumed he was still in Hawaii.

Assumed…

Yes. But Jed hadn't actually said that was where he was, had he? In fact he had really only said it must be a brief telephone call because he didn't have a lot of time. Because he'd been in a hurry to get back to Mia Douglas…?

She didn't understand. Admittedly, Jed had been gone almost a week now, but the night before his departure he had made love to her until dawn. In truth, after months of their not having made love at all, Georgie had been surprised at his ardour, but had assumed it to be because, despite the strain which had developed in their relationship just recently, he was actually as reluctant to be apart from her as she was from him.

Assumed.

There was that word again.

Maybe it hadn't been because he would miss her at

all; maybe it had been his guilty conscience because he'd already known he was going to be unfaithful to her…?

'I shouldn't take too much notice of this.' Her grandfather threw the newspaper down in disgust. 'Pure publicity, I expect.'

Georgie's gaze was drawn back to that damning photograph as if by a magnet. Jed stood smilingly next to the stunning, beautiful actress, his arm draped lightly across her shoulders, while Mia Douglas looked up at him with a definitely avaricious light in her glowing blue eyes.

'Publicity for whom?' Georgie asked her grandfather hollowly. If it were something to do with L & J Hotels…

'Mia Douglas, presumably,' her grandfather speculated.

Nothing to do with L & J Hotels, then.

Georgie looked back at the photograph, feeling sick just at the sight of Jed with another woman. How could he? How could he do this to her after all the pain and disappointment of recent months?

The caption beneath the photograph did nothing to alleviate her anxiety! 'Mia Douglas with her escort Jed Lord at a charity dinner hosted by director Hamish McCloud'.

'Her escort'… No chance meeting, then. No mistaken identity. Jed had openly accompanied the other woman to dinner—in aid of charity or otherwise!

She threw the newspaper down and stood up abruptly. 'I think I'll go up to my room.' She turned away blindly.

'Georgina!' Her grandfather halted her flight. 'I—I think it's time you and I had a little chat about…things, don't you?'

She blinked the tears away, looking across at him, perplexed. 'What things?'

'That photograph, for one thing.' He gestured grimly towards the newspaper she had discarded. 'Your marriage to Jed, for another...'

'My marriage to Jed?' she repeated guardedly. Surely Jed hadn't discussed their problems with her own grandfather?

Her grandfather grimaced. 'I did try to warn Jed when he asked my permission to marry you and we came to our arrangement. I thought perhaps you were too young, but I had hoped the marriage would prove a success nonetheless. From the way the two of you have been behaving towards each other just lately I can only conclude that I was wrong,' he finished regretfully.

Georgie sat down suddenly; what 'arrangement'? 'Go on,' she invited breathlessly.

Her grandfather gave a disgusted snort. 'It obviously isn't working at all, is it!'

'Isn't it?' She was still guarded.

'You know it isn't.' Her grandfather sighed. 'Do you think that I haven't noticed the way the two of you no longer spend any time together? That you're only politely civil to each other? Of course I've noticed those things, Georgina. You know I'm right—otherwise you wouldn't be here and Jed—somewhere else.'

With another woman, he could have added, but didn't—although the implication was there nonetheless.

But it was his previous statement that held Georgie's attention. What arrangement had her grandfather been talking about?

'He's away on hotel business,' she said lamely.

Her grandfather didn't seem impressed. 'He doesn't work twenty-four hours a day—'

'Obviously not,' Georgie snapped back with an angrily pointed look at the open newspaper.

Her grandfather looked across at her with raised brows. 'What did you expect, Georgina? Jed is a normal red-blooded man, with all the needs that go along with that.'

She knew exactly how physically passionate her husband could be! At least…she had. 'That doesn't excuse—'

'It's a wife's place to be with her husband,' her grandfather pointed out grimly. 'Especially when that wife doesn't have the ties of her own work.'

Georgie tried to defend herself. 'Jed has never asked me to go with him.' But even as she said it she knew that wasn't completely true.

When they'd first been married Jed had often asked her to go with him when he had to go away on business, and for a while she had done exactly that. But not recently. Not for eighteen months, to be exact.

Because it was round about then that the strain had developed in their marriage. A strain they had recently learnt was insurmountable…

'Or children that would keep her tied closer to the home,' her grandfather continued, as if she hadn't spoken.

The insurmountable problem.

Because, after months of medical checks and tests, Georgie had learned that the likelihood of her ever having a child, of giving Jed a child of his own, was extremely remote.

A fact neither Georgie or Jed had yet chosen to confide in anyone else...

She bristled resentfully at her grandfather's obvious criticism. 'I do have a life of my own to live, Grandfather—'

'Lunches and coffee with old schoolfriends,' he dismissed scathingly.

Her cheeks became flushed. 'It may not be your idea of a life, Grandfather, but—'

'It most certainly isn't.' Her grandfather stood up impatiently. 'Obviously it isn't Jed's either.'

'I don't care whether Jed—' She broke off her angry reply, breathing deeply in her agitation.

'Whether Jed...?' her grandfather prompted softly.

She shot him a resentful glance. 'Grandfather, you said a few minutes ago that you had a hand in our marriage. You mentioned some sort of arrangement,' she reminded him stiffly.

'Maybe so,' he agreed. 'But I did it with the best intentions. You and Jed seemed happy enough when you were first married. But just recently... What went wrong, Georgie?'

What went wrong?

What had gone right!

She had married Jed because she loved him. But over a period of time it had occurred to her that he had never said those words back to her. As the weeks then months passed, with Georgie trying in every way she could to find out exactly what Jed felt towards her, she had come to the conclusion that it certainly wasn't love.

But they were married, and Georgie was very much

in love with Jed—so much so that she had hoped a child might bring them emotionally closer.

But even that wasn't to be. After almost a year of trying she had persuaded Jed to visit a doctor with her to find out why she wasn't conceiving.

They had received the results from those tests to find that Georgie was the one with the problem.

If anything the strain between Jed and herself had become even worse, with the result that Georgie felt completely inadequate as a woman and, as such, unwanted by Jed. So much so that she had started to avoid being with him whenever she could.

A fact her grandfather had obviously been only too well aware of!

But there was still her grandfather's puzzling comment about his own arrangement with Jed concerning their having got married at all...

It most certainly hadn't been an arrangement on her part, but was that how Jed viewed their marriage? With Georgie as George's only heir, and Jed as Estelle's, their marriage was yet another cementing together of the Lord and Jones families—keeping the L & J Group completely within that family circle. After all, Jed had never once claimed to love her.

With a sickening jolt of her stomach Georgie realised that at last she had the answer to the puzzle of Jed's feelings towards her. Now she knew that the reason Jed had never told her he loved her was because he didn't, he never had. He had only married her at all to prevent her marrying someone outside the family.

With or without her grandfather's collusion...?

One glance at the hard determination in her grandfather's face had been enough to answer that question; her grandfather was the one who had claimed earlier that her marriage to Jed was an 'arrangement', and Georgie realised now that that was exactly what it was—a business arrangement between the two men! Obviously her own feelings in the matter hadn't been important to either of them.

Except Georgie had now foiled that arrangement by being incapable of providing the Lord-Jones heir…

All this time she had believed in her grandfather's love for her, dismissing all those people who had claimed he was a hard-headed businessman who allowed nothing and no one to stand in his way once he had made up his mind to do something.

Looking at him now, at the hard determination in his face, she realised that all this time she was the one who had totally under-estimated him…!

And Jed…

She stiffened, rising slowly to her feet, her movements measured as she forced herself to remain calm, not to give in to the scream of protest raging inside her to break free at the enormity of what these two men—two men she had loved absolutely—had tried to do to her.

'You're right, Grandfather. My marriage to Jed is a disaster,' she told him evenly. 'So much so that I've decided I don't wish to go on with it any longer.'

'You don't wish—' His cheeks became mottled with suppressed anger. 'Georgina, surely this is something you need to discuss with Jed when he—'

'I said *I've* decided, Grandfather,' she cut in forcefully. 'Which means I have no intention of discussing it with Jed—when he comes home or at any other time in the future.' Her voice hardened angrily.

'You're just over-reacting to the photograph of Jed in the newspaper with another woman,' he cajoled.

But Georgie was adamant. 'My decision has nothing to do with that photograph in the newspaper. It's something I've been thinking about for some time.'

'Look, Georgina, don't do anything when you're upset like this.' Her grandfather attempted to soothe her. 'I realise it must have been a disappointment to you to discover there will never be a child, but—'

'Jed has *told* you that I can't have children?' she gasped, feeling nauseous at the thought of Jed's complete betrayal.

'Of course,' her grandfather confirmed. 'It's something that you couldn't keep a secret for ever, Georgina,' he added placatingly as he saw how pale she had become. 'And poor Jed—'

'Yes—poor Jed,' she echoed. She had thought she couldn't be hurt any more than she already was after learning of Jed's duplicity in marrying her at all, but to learn that he had discussed her inability to conceive with her grandfather—and she could only guess at the reason he had felt the need to do that!—without even discussing it with her first was the biggest betrayal of all as far as she was concerned.

'He had to talk to someone, Georgina,' her grandfather reasoned chidingly.

'Of course he did,' she dismissed scathingly. 'I'm sorry I've proved such a disappointment to you, Grandfather. But I'm sure my decision will only make things awkward for a short time. You and Jed will soon come to some other "arrangement" that will suit you both. If it helps the situation at all, I can assure you I will be making no future claim on anyone or anything to do with L & J Hotels.'

'You—'

'I mean it, Grandfather,' she assured him hardly. 'With any luck I will have moved out before Jed gets back. But, I state again, I will be making no claims on any of you.'

'But—'

'Of any kind,' she continued determinedly. 'Financial or otherwise.'

He frowned darkly at this. 'But how will you live?'

'I have my legacy from my parents, and—well, I'm sure there must be something I'm good at. After all, I'm obviously no good at being a wife or mother,' she added emotionally.

The pain of knowing how much these two men had betrayed her, and her love for them both, she would deal with later. Much later. Once she was well away from here. And them.

'Georgina—'

'Please don't, Grandfather.' She cut him short as he would have reached out to her. 'I think it's best if I go now, don't you?' she reasoned. 'Please tell Jed when he returns that my lawyer will contact him concerning our divorce.'

'Divorce?' Her grandfather looked startled. 'Georgina, you're not giving this enough thought—'

'I've thought of nothing but the disaster my marriage is almost since its conception,' she assured him honestly.

She had known from the beginning that there was

something seriously wrong with her relationship with Jed, that all the love seemed to be on her side. As far as she was concerned, knowing the reason she had felt that way completely exonerated her from any responsibility to either of these men—emotionally or in any other way.

'I will tell Jed of my decision on his return,' she told her grandfather flatly.

'As long as you realise he isn't going to take that decision lightly,' her grandfather warned her.

'Oh, I think he'll be more than happy to agree to the divorce once he realises the freedom it will give him.' The freedom to choose a woman who could give him the children needed to continue the Lord line! 'In the meantime, I'm going upstairs to pack my things before returning to our apartment.' Where she intended packing all her other things and having them put into storage while she searched for somewhere of her own to live.

By the time Jed returned home he would probably be gratified to realise it was almost as if she had never been in his life at all...

Georgie blinked back the tears as she remembered all too clearly the pain and disillusion she had known two years ago as she returned to their apartment and packed away her marriage to Jed into several large cartons.

That day hadn't been the end of it, of course. There had been several heated scenes with Jed once he returned and finally managed to track her down to the hotel where she was staying temporarily while she looked for an apartment of her own. Not one of the L & J group, of course!

But despite Jed's anger Georgie had remained adamant about never returning to him or the marriage that she now considered a complete sham. Finally Jed had agreed to accept their separation, and the signing of their divorce papers six months ago had been a mere technicality. On Jed's part there had never been any real marriage to divorce from, and Georgie had long since made a new life for herself—one that didn't include Jed or her grandfather.

But none of those painful memories brought her any closer to understanding her feelings of jealousy today concerning Jed's date with Sukie Lawson. Or explain why Jed had just kissed her in the way that he had...

She was still in this state of confusion later that evening when she picked up the telephone and found it was Jed at the other end of the line!

'What do you want?' she questioned suspiciously as she instantly recognised his voice. 'And how did you get this telephone number?' she added accusingly.

'Obviously I want to talk to you,' Jed returned lazily. 'And I've had this telephone number for some weeks, Georgie.'

'Some weeks...!' she echoed, wondering exactly how he had obtained her ex-directory number. But of course he was Jed Lord, with the contacts to find out anything he might want to know. 'But—then why didn't you just telephone me to let me know about Estelle's illness?' Instead of going through that elaborate charade at the Lawsons' on Friday evening...?

But she already knew the answer to that question. Jed had gone through that elaborate charade for no other reason than that he wanted to—because Jed never did anything he didn't want to! The real question was, why had he wanted to meet her at the Lawsons at all…?

'Too easy,' he explained derisively. 'I'm on my way over to your apartment right now, Georgie,' he continued briskly. 'Make sure your watchdog of a doorman knows to let me in, hmm?'

'I— But—' She was babbling! 'I don't want you here, Jed,' she told him forcefully, her hand tightly gripping the telephone receiver in her agitation.

She couldn't bear to have him here in her apartment, to have the memory of him in any part of her new life; it was bad enough that she would wonder in the future, every time she went to the Lawsons', whether or not she might bump into Jed there, without having the memory of his overwhelming presence in her apartment too!

'Too bad,' he replied. 'Because I need to speak to you. And I need to do it now,' he stated harshly as she would have protested once again. 'Unless, of course, Lawson is already there…?' he added softly.

'As it happens, Andrew isn't here this evening,' Georgie informed him. She had arranged to meet Andrew tomorrow evening, unsure how she was going to feel after visiting her grandfather's home today. As it happened, bearing in mind her earlier confusion, it had been a good decision. 'But he does have a perfect right to be here if he chooses to be,' she defended.

'Unlike me, hmm?' Jed murmured appreciatively.

'Yes!' she confirmed swiftly.

'Nevertheless, I will be there in five minutes, Georgie,' Jed told her. 'I don't expect there to be any problem about my being allowed in,' he said pointedly, before ending the call.

Or else, his tone clearly implied, Georgie realised frustratedly as she slowly replaced her own handset.

Never mind that she didn't want him here. Never mind that he was intruding on her privacy. Never mind that he was totally aware of all that—Jed was on his way to her apartment and that was the end of the subject.

That was what he thought!

CHAPTER NINE

'NICE,' Jed murmured appreciatively as he stepped out of the lift straight into the outer hallway of Georgie's apartment.

Georgie knew he had to be talking about the elegance of her apartment and not her; she was looking most unelegant herself, in the faded denims and over-large rugby shirt that she wore at weekends when doing her housework! Her face was bare of make-up too, and she had just briefly run her fingers through her hair.

In truth, she had deliberately not made any effort concerning her own appearance—had no intention of letting Jed think for one moment that his visit here this evening was anything more than an inconvenience.

Jed, however, was still wearing the casual clothes he'd had on when he went out earlier to meet Sukie Lawson for lunch, posing the question: had he been home at all since lunchtime?

Probably not, Georgie decided as she looked at him coldly. 'What do you want, Jed?'

He calmly returned her hostile gaze. 'You asked me that earlier, and I seem to remember I told you I want to talk to you,' he replied tersely.

'So—talk,' she invited rudely.

Jed frowned darkly, grey eyes opaquely silver. Evidence that, no matter how coldly aloof he might seem on the outside, inside he was actually extremely angry.

Well, that was just too bad—because Georgie was angry too. And as far as she was concerned with more reason!

Jed drew in a deeply controlling breath. 'Invite me in, Georgie, and I just might do that,' he drawled.

'I—'

'You're looking good, by the way,' he observed lightly.

Georgie gave him a withering glance. 'You're talking rubbish, Jed—and we both know it!'

'No, we don't,' he rebuked mildly. 'You look—relaxed, comfortable, completely natural. Beautiful, in fact. In the past you always tried too hard,' he told her as she would have spoken.

'I'm so sorry!' she answered with complete insincerity. 'I'll have to remember in the future that the scruffy look is what appeals to you—and make sure I'm always extremely smart in your presence!' She glared at him.

Jed grinned, obviously not at all put out by her annoyance. 'Please yourself,' he said. 'I like your hair in that style too, by the way,' he added huskily.

At last he had mentioned her change of hairstyle—but not at all in the way Georgie had expected. 'You never used to be this complimentary, Jed,' she derided.

He grimaced. 'I never used to be a lot of things,' he responded. 'Are you going to ask me in or not?' he persisted.

'Not,' Georgie came back instantly, crossing her arms in front of her to look at him challengingly.

'That isn't very friendly of you, Georgie—'

'We aren't friends!' she snapped.

'I've only come here to do you a favour,' he continued firmly.

'A favour?' Georgie echoed. 'For me? Somehow I don't see that happening!'

His mouth thinned, his eyes narrowing. 'If you don't invite me in you'll never know, will you.'

Georgie glared at him frustratedly, half of her wanting to tell him to go to hell, the other half curious as to what he could possibly have to say to her that would be doing her a favour. And along with that latter curiosity she had the fact that she really didn't want to invite him further inside her apartment...

She gave a rueful smile. 'I think I can live without knowing, so if you wouldn't mind——?'

'Sukie Lawson knows I was in your bedroom on Friday evening,' Jed cut across her.

'You told her about it?' Georgie gasped accusingly; she hadn't believed that even Jed would——

'No, I didn't tell her about it,' he barked impatiently. 'Damn it, Georgie, when are you going to stop believing my greatest pleasure in life is to cause you as much discomfort as possible?'

'Maybe when you stop enjoying watching me squirm!'

Jed sighed, shaking his head. 'I have never enjoyed watching you squirm,' he rejoined tersely. 'Now, stop being so damned inhospitable and let's go and talk about this situation with Sukie Lawson,' he instructed irritably.

'You're the one who has a ''situation'' with Sukie,' Georgie told him.

'Will you stop letting your prejudice show where I'm concerned and actually try listening to what I'm saying to you?' Jed rasped impatiently. 'Personally, it's of no interest to me if Andrew Lawson finds out I was in your bedroom on Friday evening—but I had a feeling that it might be of interest you!'

And he was right. Of course he was right. She was just having difficulty coping with the fact that Jed was here at all. But of course she had to hear what Sukie had said to him about Friday evening—if only so that she had an answer ready for Andrew if, or when, he should ask her about it! Brother and sister weren't close and never had been, but Sukie was still an unknown quantity to Georgie—as was what she might actually do with the information concerning Jed's visit to her bedroom...

'Okay, you had better come in,' she invited ungraciously, pushing open the door behind her that led straight into the sitting room of her apartment, preceding him into the room but turning so that she could gauge his reaction to her rather Bohemian style of decor.

There were no carpets on the highly polished wood floors, just scatter rugs. Several heavy chairs and sofas were placed about the room, with colourful throws over them, and an abundance of plants and flowers cascaded down walls and furniture. One wall of the room was completely shelved, with books overflowing from those shelves onto the floor. The whole effect was one of comfort rather than style—a haven of rusticity that Georgie was sometimes very loath to leave.

'This is great, Georgie!' Jed looked about him admiringly, his response too natural to be anything other than genuine.

She gave a perplexed frown, remembering all too clearly the symmetry and minimalist style of the apartment she and Jed had shared when they were married. Jed had brought in an interior designer to transform the rooms into places of cool elegance. As a place to entertain it had been perfect; as a place where Georgie could actually live in relaxed comfort it had failed utterly, its expensive elegance only adding to her misery.

'Glad you like it,' she returned with dry scepticism.

Jed turned back to her, head tilted to one side as he looked at her dispassionately. 'You don't believe me, do you?' he guessed ruefully. 'If I were to tell you that I wish we had made a success of our marriage, would you believe that either?' He studied her from between narrowed lids.

'No,' Georgie answered unhesitantly, her expression hurt.

'Hmm.' He grimaced thoughtfully. 'Well, what if I were to tell you that—?'

'Jed, could you just get to the point?' she snapped, her nerves already stretched to breaking point. It was bad enough having him here at all, without his prolonging the occasion with these ridiculous comments.

'The point...?' He frowned. 'Oh, yes,' he realised. 'Aren't you going to offer me a sociable drink?'

She shook her head. 'This isn't a social call.'

'But—'

'Ex-husbands do not pay social calls on their ex-wives!' Georgie retorted.

'Who says they don't?' he mused.

'Jed!' she cried.

Lunch was pretty unappetising, and I've had nothing to eat or drink since that time, so I think it would be only good manners if you were to—'

'Okay!' Georgie held up defensive hands. 'One cup of coffee. And then you leave,' she advised warningly. Anything to get him to say what he had to say and then just go!

'I would prefer a whisky, if you have some,' he requested lightly as he sat down in one of the hugely comfortable armchairs. 'I don't have anywhere else to drive this evening, so—'

'You have to drive home!' Georgie reminded him forcefully, but moved to pour the whisky into a glass anyway; now that he had made himself comfortable she doubted that Jed would move until he got what he wanted. And he knew very well that she had some whisky in the apartment; the nearly full bottle was on clear view on the dresser.

'Only around the corner,' Jed replied. 'I can easily stay at my own apartment tonight. I moved out of our place a year ago,' he explained at her questioning look. 'When it became obvious you weren't coming back. It's amazing, really; we've been living almost next door to each other for the last year.'

What was she supposed to say to that? Oh, goody? Wonderful? What a marvellous coincidence?

Well, if that was what Jed expected he was going to be disappointed, because she wasn't going to say any of those things. She was more interested in the remark he had made just before that; what did he mean, when it had become obvious she wasn't coming back? After the way they had parted he couldn't possibly have believed she would ever go back to him or their marriage—could he?

'Here you are.' She handed him the glass with its half

an inch of whisky in the bottom. A fact that Jed noted with a mocking rise of dark brows. 'You still need to be sober to walk home,' she told him firmly, sitting down in the armchair that faced his.

'You're a hard woman, Georgie,' he joked, before sipping the fiery liquid. 'I almost took up drinking this as a hobby after you left me,' he continued conversationally.

Georgie felt very uncomfortable with these references to their past relationship. 'Before you realised you still had all the things you had before you married me—your work, the grandparents, your freedom,' she pointed out.

Jed looked across at her consideringly. 'But not you,' he murmured softly. 'Aren't you joining me?' He indicated the glass in his hand.

She shook her head. 'I've never liked whisky.' Although she *was* tempted to go and pour herself a glass of wine from the bottle she had open in the cooler, Jed didn't look as if he were in any sort of hurry to leave, and she was finding this conversation more and more disturbing; she and Jed had never talked together like this in the past.

'Sukie?' she reminded him.

'Hmm,' he said. 'Apparently she was on her way to her bedroom on Friday evening—'

'You're sure she was on her way to her own bedroom?' Georgie couldn't stop herself from taunting.

Jed shot her an impatient glance. 'Georgie, I have never slept with Sukie Lawson. Have no intention of ever sleeping with Sukie Lawson. Do not feel the least attraction towards Sukie Lawson. Clear enough for you?' he grated harshly.

'Very,' she replied. 'But you went out with her for lunch today—'

'At her invitation, not mine,' Jed quickly explained. 'We met at breakfast yesterday morning—something you and Andrew Lawson noticeably missed, by the way.'

Georgie tried not to rise to his bait. 'Don't you remember, Jed? I rarely eat breakfast,' she said calmly.

'And Andrew Lawson?'

'I have no idea,' she dismissed, meeting his gaze unflinchingly. 'So, you and Sukie met at breakfast yesterday morning…?' she reminded him.

He nodded tersely. 'She invited me out for lunch today.'

'But you didn't have to accept,' Georgie observed.

Jed looked serious. 'She implied she had something important she wanted to discuss with me. Besides, it would have been extremely rude to have refused, in the circumstances.'

Georgie shot him a sceptical glance. 'So, Sukie was on her way to her bedroom on Friday evening…?' she prompted—yet again. Really, Jed used to be more concise than this!

He took a leisurely sip of his whisky. 'She heard voices in the guest bedroom—your guest bedroom—'

'Wouldn't it have been natural to assume—in the circumstances—that my nocturnal visitor was Andrew, and just move on?' Georgie derided.

Jed shot her a look of dark irritation. 'Maybe,' he replied. 'But she obviously didn't think so. She saw me leaving your bedroom a few minutes later.'

'On her way to…?'

'Nowhere.' Jed's mouth twisted. 'She was honest enough to admit she hung around in the hallway waiting to see exactly who was visiting you at that time of night. A little shocked at the thought of her younger brother misbehaving right there in their parents' home, probably.'

Georgie winced with distaste at the mere thought of Sukie watching outside her bedroom in that way. 'She must have found it well worth the wait then, when it turned out to be you who left and not Andrew! What explanation did you give her today for having been in my bedroom Friday evening?'

'Ah,' he said.

'Ah, what?' Georgie exclaimed. 'Jed, you did give her an explanation?' she demanded incredulously.

'Of a sort. You have to realise, Georgie, I was thrown slightly off-balance by the question. I had no time to come up with any other answer than—'

'The truth?' Georgie said, jumping impatiently to her feet to glare down at him. 'You told Sukie Lawson that the two of us were once married to each other?' She glared at him accusingly. 'Jed, how could you—?'

'Of course I didn't tell the woman that,' he responded, sitting forward on the edge of his chair to place his empty whisky glass down on the coffee table. 'Give me credit for having a little sensitivity, okay!'

She gave a pained wince. 'But if you didn't tell Sukie the truth, what did you tell her?' Georgie had a distinct feeling she wasn't going to like the answer to this particular question.

Jed looked up, grinning, grey eyes alight with devilish

humour. 'That I was attracted to you. That I went to your bedroom to try to proposition you!'

'You—' Georgie broke off, absolutely astounded by this explanation. 'You told Sukie *what*?' she finally managed to burst out.

'That I went to your bedroom to try to proposition you,' Jed repeated vaguely, his gaze caught and held by something behind her. He stood up to walk past her in the direction of the bookcases against the far wall. 'I've been trying to get this book for weeks now.' He took a hardback book off one of the shelves, opening it up to read the fly-leaf. 'Have you read it yet?' he asked distractedly.

'As a matter of fact, yes,' she answered, a little surprised that Jed, of all people, should have been trying to get a copy of that particular book. 'Jed, you told Andrew's sister that—'

'Yes,' he confirmed impatiently. 'Is it any good?' He held up the book.

'Excellent,' she responded. 'Jed, you told Andrew's sister—'

'You already said that.' He sighed. 'And I've already said that, yes, I did. Is it as good as the rest in the series?' He held the book up.

'Yes, it is.' Georgie was becoming more and more incredulous by the minute.

The book Jed was holding was the fifth in a very popular children's series. Over a period of years it had become popular with adults too, each successive book taking the country by storm and heading the bestseller list; Georgie just hadn't expected Jed to be one of those adults who read them...

'Can I borrow it?' he enquired expectantly.

'No! Yes! I don't know,' she rejoined in complete confusion. 'What did Sukie say after you told her that?'

'Well, as I had rebuffed all *her* advances—Friday evening as well as today—she was probably relieved to know it wasn't her brother I was attracted to! Okay, okay.' Jed held up pacifying hands as Georgie's anger visibly grew. 'So, I told Sukie that—would you rather I *had* told her the truth?'

'No,' she said. But neither was she happy about her future sister-in-law thinking she had let a man other than Andrew into her bedroom on Friday evening.

After all, it was hardly the time of night for anyone to be paying a purely social call! And Jed had already told Sukie that he was attracted to her, which pretty well took care of Georgie trying to use that excuse herself when she next spoke to the other woman...

'Besides,' Jed went on, putting down the book he was holding to look at her with eyes that were suddenly opaquely grey, 'it was the truth.'

'What was?' Georgie said, not sure quite what he meant.

She was lost in thought about what she could say to Andrew if his sister chose to tell him about Jed's nocturnal visit to her bedroom; she certainly wasn't about to confirm to Andrew that it had been because Jed was attracted to her—

Georgie looked up suddenly, eyeing Jed suspiciously as his words—if not their meaning!—finally registered. 'What did you just say?' she said slowly.

'I wish you would pay attention, Georgie,' Jed drawled. 'I said it was the truth,' he told her evenly.

Georgie frowned uncomprehendingly. 'And I said, What was?' she reminded him.

'So you did,' Jed agreed, taking a step towards her. 'It's true that I find you attractive, Georgie,' he said quietly. 'In fact, I find you very attractive.'

She stared at him, sure that he couldn't have said what he just had, and that if he had he couldn't really have meant it.

Could he…?

CHAPTER TEN

GEORGIE stared up at him. 'Jed, you and I were married…'

'Yes,' he confirmed.

'To each other!' she added.

'Yes,' he acknowledged with a rueful quirk of his mouth.

Georgie's confusion deepened. 'But now we're divorced,' she reminded him.

Jed sobered. 'Unfortunately, the answer to that statement is also—yes.'

Georgie eyed him frustratedly. 'Divorce implies a little incompatibility—if not a lot!—of incompatibility!'

'You were the one who divorced me,' Jed reminded her softly.

'Exactly! Which implies, if nothing else, that—'

'It implies that you wanted to divorce me, Georgie,' Jed cut in evenly. 'It does not imply that I felt the same way about you.'

'But— But—' She broke off, realising she was starting to sound like an old engine that wouldn't start! 'You agreed to the divorce,' she recalled.

'At the time your grandfather advised that it would probably be the wisest course—'

'My grandfather?' Georgie repeated in astonishment. 'But he told me he doesn't believe in divorce!'

'Exactly,' Jed said with satisfaction.

'I don't understand any of this,' she said, running a trembling hand over her brow, feeling completely puzzled and befuddled—but then, when had she ever been anything else where Jed's emotions were concerned?

'You wanted a divorce, Georgie, so I agreed to let you have one,' Jed told her. 'That doesn't necessarily mean I wanted to divorce you, though, does it?'

No, it didn't. But she had thought— 'Jed, we had been living apart for eighteen months by the time I applied for our divorce.'

'Yes,' he acknowledged.

'You agreed,' she pressured.

'I've just told you why I did that,' Jed reasoned.

Georgie gave a frustrated shake of her head. 'Are you now telling me that you didn't want a divorce from me?'

'Not only am I telling you that,' he replied, 'but I'm also of the same opinion as your grandfather when it comes to divorce—I don't recognize it, Georgie!'

'But—' No, she would not sound like that stalling engine again! 'No matter whether you recognise it or not, Jed, we *are* divorced,' she assured him firmly. 'A judge said so. The law says so. *I* say so,' she added determinedly.

Jed gave a considering inclination of his head. 'I doubt you would have become engaged to another man if you didn't truly believe you were free to do so,' he responded calmly.

'Well, then—'

'Well, then nothing!' Jed suddenly came back, taking another step towards her. 'Georgie—'

'I thought Grandie seemed a little—better when I visited her today.' She desperately latched onto another subject—in an effort to give herself time to catch up with this one!

She and Jed had rowed very badly when she'd told him she wouldn't be coming back to their apartment to live with him. They had barely spoken for almost a year after that, and following that time all communication had been through their respective lawyers. Jed had signed the divorce papers, for goodness' sake—he couldn't just suddenly decide to change his mind about that now!

Although, if he were to be believed, he wasn't claiming to have changed his mind about anything—was very firmly stating that he hadn't wanted the divorce in the first place. Not only that, he was claiming he didn't recognise it!

Well, *she* recognised it—and that was all that mattered!

'Grandie?' Jed echoed now, his gaze narrowing.

'Yes,' Georgie confirmed hurriedly. 'She's still physically very frail, obviously. But I'm sure I detected a spark of her old indomitable self today as we talked together. She's not at all happy with you, by the way, for just disappearing in the way that you did,' she told him, sure Estelle would be having words with her grandson later today.

'Georgie, ordinarily I would be quite happy to discuss my grandmother's progress with you, just not now, hmm?' he prompted chidingly. 'Why did you become engaged to Lawson, Georgie?'

'Why?' she said dazedly, once again completely unprepared for this frontal attack on her personal life; so much for trying to divert Jed's attention onto something else! 'Because I love him, of course. Because I intend marrying him!'

Jed stood inches away from her now, giving her a considering look. 'Are you absolutely sure about that?' he finally pressed.

Georgie swallowed hard, knowing that she would be lying—to herself!—if she didn't inwardly acknowledge that she was deeply disturbed by Jed's close proximity.

He was so close now she could see the black flecks in the grey of his eyes, could see every pore of his skin, could smell the aftershave that she knew she would always associate with him, could feel the heat given off by his body. A body she was intimately familiar with...

Should she be this aware of Jed when she was engaged to marry another man...?

More to the point, should she be engaged to Andrew, even thinking of marrying him, when she was this aware of Jed, the man who had once been her husband?

She had a feeling that the answer to that was no...

She straightened defensively, at the same time meeting Jed's searching gaze unflinchingly. 'Yes, I'm sure about that,' she told him firmly. 'Now, if you wouldn't mind, it's very late—'

'What reason do you intend giving Lawson for my having been in your bedroom on Friday evening?' Jed put in softly.

Reminding her all too forcefully that she would probably have to give that in the very near future! Not only would she have to explain Jed's presence in her bedroom, she would also have to explain that he had once been her husband. Once she had admitted to the latter, was Andrew going to believe any explanation she made about the former…?

'His name is Andrew,' she returned smartly, angry with Jed all over again for having put her in this defensive position. 'And what I choose to tell Andrew—about anything—is my own business.'

'Your book is selling very well, I believe.' Jed changed the subject.

'My book…?' Georgie scrabbled mentally to catch up.

'Yes,' Jed said. 'I hear sales are going very well, and that when your second book is published early next year there's even talk of a—'

'You hear, Jed?' Georgie exploded indignantly. How on earth did he know these things?

'—of a book-signing tour,' Jed completed calmly.

Her cheeks became flushed. 'You hear correctly,' she bit out resentfully. Never mind how he had found out these things about her book. He was Jed Lord; he could find out anything if he chose to do so!

Jed seemed unconcerned. 'No doubt there will be reporters present at some of those book-signings? Nowadays the public seems to have an interest in not only reading the books, but learning more about the personal life of—'

'Your point, Jed?' she cut in impatiently—although she had a feeling she already knew what that point was going to be.

Oh, why hadn't she just told Andrew the truth from the beginning—admitted to having been married and divorced? It would have saved all the trouble she was having on the subject now. Although she wasn't sure having to admit Jed Lord had been her husband wasn't damning enough on its own!

'I'm sure you already know what that is, Georgie,' Jed suggested gently. 'What you choose to tell Lawson about me and our marriage is probably going to be totally irrelevant after your book-signing tour next year. The press is going to be all over you once they realise exactly who author Georgie Jones is!'

'The ex-wife of Jed Lord?' she snorted.

He shook his head. 'The granddaughter of George Jones—founder and co-owner of the L & J Group.'

Her cheeks flushed even more. 'But also the ex-wife of Jed Lord, his obvious successor,' she persisted.

He gave a rueful grimace. 'Yes.'

She had always known that there was a possibility her connection to both George and Jed could come out, if her books became successful, but she had hoped by that time she and Andrew would already be married—that she would be able to explain the past calmly and dismissively.

As it deserved to be explained!

She had been eighteen years old, for goodness' sake— had loved Jed all her life, it seemed; of course she had married him when he asked her. It had taken maturity to help her realise the reason he had felt compelled to ask her in the first place.

'I'll just explain that we all make mistakes,' she stated.

Jed's expression darkened. His eyes narrowed to steely slits. 'Our marriage was not a mistake, Georgie—'

'Of course it was,' she responded.

'No,' Jed countered, 'it wasn't.'

Georgie wasn't about to give in. 'We'll just have to agree to differ about that—because I have no intention of getting into an argument about it, now or at any other time. I thank you for coming here and warning me that Sukie may decide to cause trouble because of what happened on Friday evening—'

'That isn't why I'm here,' Jed interrupted her.

She gave him a startled look, moving slightly away as she saw the intensity of his gaze fixed on her parted lips. 'I— You—' She couldn't help it—her tongue moved instinctively to moisten those lips, and Jed's gaze darkened even more as he watched the movement. 'Jed—'

'Georgie…!' he groaned, even as his hands reached out to lightly grasp the tops of Georgie's arms, his head slowly lowering towards hers.

Attack, Georgie, she instructed herself. Attack—before you lost the will to do anything more than go weak at the knees!

'Strange isn't it, Jed?' she began with deliberate self-derision. 'How I ended up writing children's books and I can't have children of my own. How lucky for you, Jed, that will never change!'

Jed froze, his expression unreadable now. 'Lucky?' he echoed slowly.

Georgie nodded. 'That I'll never have a child who could challenge your sole right to the L & J Group!'

His face twisted thunderously. 'That's a hell of an accusation to make!'

'But so true,' she taunted. 'Don't you realise, Jed? You don't need me any more to achieve your goal in life—'

'You're wrong,' he denied, his hands tightening on her arms. 'You're exactly what I need to achieve my lifetime ambition. In fact,' he added, 'I can't do it without you!'

Georgie had no time to question this statement, no time to puzzle over his strange reply to her accusation—because at that moment Jed's head lowered completely to a level with hers, his lips claiming hers with a familiarity that took her breath away.

Yet, as Jed's mouth began to explore hers, Georgie realised it wasn't completely as it used to be; she was older, her self-esteem boosted by a successful career, by Andrew's complete admiration for her achievements. And she now met Jed's unmistakable passion as an equal, as someone who knew her own worth—and cherished that knowledge.

The combination was completely explosive!

Her arms became entwined about Jed's neck and she pressed closer, her body curving into the hardness of his as desire burst into consuming flame. She literally felt as if she were on fire!

All the time that meeting of lips continued. Deepened. Searched. Found. Asked. Received their reply.

Only the two of them existed, their heat, their desire, their need for each other. Georgie offered no resistance as Jed swung her up in his arms and carried her towards the open door of her bedroom, their fevered kisses continuing.

It was as if they couldn't get enough of each other. As if they had been through a drought and now wanted to drown. In each other.

It was only semi-dark as Jed placed her gently down

on top of the bed. Georgie looked up at him with complete knowledge of what she was doing. Of what she was about to do.

Jed knelt on the side of the bed, his hands reaching out to frame Georgie's face. 'You are so beautiful,' he groaned. 'So absolutely beautiful that I—'

'Please don't talk, Jed,' she begged as she reached up to pull him down to her.

She didn't want him to say anything that would spoil the perfection of this moment. Of these moments. She wanted only to belong completely to him. And for him to belong completely to her.

His lips once more claimed hers, and their clothes disappeared almost as if they had simply evaporated, until nothing divided the warmth of their naked bodies. Bodies that fitted so perfectly together they were like two halves of a whole as Jed lay down beside her.

The silver intensity of his gaze held hers as one of his hands caressed the length of her body, cupping a breast before his head lowered and moistly warm lips and tongue sipped and caressed the sensitive flesh there.

Georgie arched ecstatically against him, her fingers buried in the dark thickness of his hair as she silently pleaded for him not to stop.

She never wanted this to stop, wanted to remain like this for ever, part of Jed as he was a part of her.

He felt so good to touch, his body warm and muscled where her hands ran caressingly up and down the length of his spine, moving in butterfly movements to the hardness of his desire, touching, teasing, wanting!

'Georgie…!' Jed's head reared and he gasped weakly.

'Now, Jed,' she encouraged him, taking one of his

hands and moving it so that he should know of her readiness for him. 'Please, now!' she begged.

He was like a perfect sculpture as he rose up above her, gently nudging her legs apart to slowly, oh, so very slowly, meld his body with hers.

Even that was too much for Georgie. Her body was on fire as spasms of pleasure coursed through her, enveloping them both as she clung to Jed's shoulders in heady release.

'Steady,' Jed gasped throatily as he once again looked down at her face in the half-light. 'Not yet, Georgie,' he breathed intensely. 'Not yet!'

She lost track of time, of space, of everything that wasn't Jed, completely consumed by him, by the passion between them. Only Jed existed in her universe.

Jed took her to the end of that universe time and time again, only allowing his own pleasure when he couldn't hold back any longer, the two of them reaching higher than Georgie had ever believed it possible to go.

'Wow...!' Jed murmured dazedly as he sank down beside her, his arm about her shoulders as he cradled her against him, her head resting on the dampness of his chest.

Wow, indeed.

Georgie had never known anything like this. She felt completely satiated, her whole body tingling with awareness, every nerve-ending, every pore in her skin, attuned totally to Jed.

Jed gave a husky laugh. 'I can't believe I just said anything so ridiculous,' he said self-derisively.

Neither could Georgie, but she knew it was really just

another part of the madness that had overtaken them. Both of them.

The problem was, what did they do now?

Being with Jed like this had been wonderful, magical. But at the same time completely removed from reality. From their reality. Because nothing had really changed. Jed was still—Jed. Heir to L & J Group and her ex-husband. And she was still Georgie. Completely separate from everything connected to the L & J Group and the ex-wife of Jed Lord, who could never provide an heir to the empire he headed. The fact that their incompatibility didn't go as far as the bedroom changed none of that.

'You've gone very quiet.' Jed looked down at her through the darkness of her bedroom.

Her cheeks burned with embarrassment as she remembered the way she had cried out her pleasure, again and again, during their lovemaking.

Jed turned on his side so that he could see her properly, his arm still about her bare shoulders. 'Georgie…?' he prompted uncertainly.

What Georgie most wanted to do was pull the covers up over both of them. Their nakedness was just a reminder of their uninhibited lovemaking. Although the tingling of her body told her she wasn't going to be able to forget this time in Jed's arms even if she tried!

She swallowed hard, gazing somewhere over Jed's shoulder in an effort not to look at him directly. One glance had told her that he looked almost boyish, with his dark hair falling over his forehead, his face relaxed into lines of physical satisfaction. 'I don't know what to say,' she admitted.

Jed smoothed the hair back from her brow. 'Are you

worried about how you're going to explain this to Lawson?' he sympathised.

She hadn't given Andrew a thought the last hour or so—how could she have done when the only person she was aware of was Jed, his touching her, her touching him?

She stiffened. 'I don't think now is the time to discuss Andrew, do you?' she said; the two of them lying naked together on the bed in the languidness after their love-making really wasn't the time to talk about another man.

'Possibly not,' Jed conceded gently. 'But he does have to be told, and I wondered if you would like me to—'

'Has to be told what?' Georgie cut in, frowning up at him now.

'About us, of course,' Jed answered quizzically.

Georgie's frown deepened. Of course she had to break her engagement to Andrew—couldn't in all conscience even consider marrying him after what had happened here this evening. But surely that was completely up to her, had nothing to do with any 'us'…?

She felt more in need than ever of the bedcovers that unfortunately lay beneath them. 'Jed, I really don't think now is the time to talk about this.'

'But I want to tell your grandfather and Grandie about us as soon as possible—'

'You want to *what*?' Georgie sat up abruptly, pushing away from Jed to swing her legs over the side of the bed and sit up, her back towards him now.

'They're going to be so pleased, Georgie—'

'Jed!' she cried. 'I don't know what you think happened here this evening, but I can assure you it isn't something you should tell our grandparents about; I'm sure they would be very shocked.'

She was shocked. And dismayed. Had no idea how she and Jed were going to even pretend at a relationship between them in front of Estelle in the future.

'Are you joking?' he exclaimed. 'They will be over the moon when we tell them we're back together!'

Georgie stood up abruptly, no longer concerned with her nakedness—although she picked up her robe from the chair and pulled it on anyway, tightly tying the belt about the slenderness of her waist before turning back to face Jed.

He sat up in the bed too now. 'We *are* back together, Georgie.' Jed's words were a statement, not a question.

'No,' she denied. 'No, we're not, Jed,' she added more firmly. 'What happened—just now—' She gave a dismissive wave of her hand in the direction of the rumpled bed. 'It didn't mean anything, Jed—' She broke off as he surged to his feet, his expression so fierce she instinctively took a step backwards.

His mouth twisted angrily. 'Don't worry, Georgie, I'm not going to touch you,' he said. 'I'm too angry to risk it,' he admitted harshly. 'What do you mean, our lovemaking didn't mean anything?' he rasped, grey eyes glittering silver.

She hesitated. 'I believe it often happens—like that—when two people were once married to each other. It's—it's called post-marital—'

'I don't want to hear what some so-called expert calls it!' Jed burst in coldly. 'I said it was lovemaking because that's what it was.'

Georgie gave a deep sigh. 'Perhaps,' she conceded. 'But—'

'No perhaps. No buts.' Jed gave an abrupt shake of his head. 'We made love with each other, Georgie! Doesn't that mean anything to you?'

She thrust her hands into the pockets of her robe, her shoulders hunched. 'I've already explained that I think it was regrettable, that it only serves to make this situation more difficult. But maybe in the circumstances it was inevitable,' she allowed. 'I believe it's called unfinished marital business—a need to—'

'Georgie, will you kindly stop quoting rubbish from some tacky magazine article you've obviously read on the subject?' Jed cut in scathingly, sitting down on the bed to begin pulling on his clothes.

Clothes that, like hers, were scattered haphazardly over the bedroom carpet!

Georgie bent down and picked up his shirt from where it lay at her feet, holding it out to him gingerly, careful not to get too close; she might be trying to sound calm and sensible about this whole sorry mess, but that didn't mean she was immune to the attraction of his nakedness—that she didn't feel the same yearning of an hour ago to lose herself in their desire for each other.

'Thanks,' he said shortly as he took the shirt. 'So, what you're saying, Georgie, is that our time together just now was just some—need on your part, to see if I was still attracted to you enough to go to bed with you?'

'I said no such thing!' she burst out resentfully. 'Why *did* you make love with me, Jed?' she challenged angrily.

'At this moment in time, in all honesty, I have absolutely no idea!' He stood up, fully dressed now. 'I think I should leave now, don't you? Before either of us says something the other will find completely unforgivable?' he offered heavily.

'Yes,' Georgie agreed, looking at him regretfully, desperately hoping her inner misery wasn't apparent on her face.

She didn't want him to go, didn't want them to part like this. But she knew there was nothing else they could do. There was no going back to their relationship before this evening, but there was no future for them either...

'Fine,' Jed said tersely, striding over to the doorway, pausing before leaving the bedroom. 'I—I hope this won't prevent you from visiting Grandie? She seems so much better.'

'No, of course not,' Georgie assured him distantly, once again unable to look at him, her shoulders even more hunched as she fought the need to stop him from leaving.

'I'll go, then,' he stated.

She swallowed hard. 'Yes.'

She didn't see him leave, but she was nevertheless aware that he was no longer in the bedroom with her. That awareness was confirmed a few seconds later with the arrival and then departure of the lift. Jed was on his way down to ground level.

All Georgie's strength deserted her and she sank down onto the carpeted floor, tears falling hotly down her cheeks as she felt her heart breaking for the second time.

Because no matter what she might have said to Jed, no matter how she had excused what had happened between them, she knew in her heart that she had made love with Jed for one reason and one reason only.

She was still in love with the man who had once been her husband!

And he was no more in love with her than he had been two years ago…!

CHAPTER ELEVEN

'How are things between you and Jed?'

Georgie looked up from the newspaper she had been reading so that she could read articles aloud for Estelle's benefit, to find her step-grandmother looking back at her concernedly.

'How are things between Jed and me?' she repeated, playing for time. What on earth could she truthfully reply to that?

Since that Sunday evening four weeks ago, when the two of them had made the mistake of going to bed together, Georgie couldn't honestly say she had seen much of Jed. But perhaps that was telling enough in itself to know how things were between them!

'Fine,' she answered firmly. 'Jed's very busy, of course. But then, so am I. Did I tell you my editor has just approved my second book—?'

'Georgie, I know I've been ill.' Estelle smiled gently. 'But I'm not senile!'

Georgie's eyes widened. 'Well, of course you aren't. Who on earth—?'

'You and Jed.' Estelle grimaced. 'There is no reconciliation, is there?'

It was so unexpected, so completely out of the blue, that Georgie could only stare at the older woman, wondering which one of them—her grandfather, Jed, or herself—by something they had done or said, had given the game away. No doubt Jed would claim it was her fault anyway!

Despite the awkwardness that now existed between Jed and herself, Georgie had continued to visit Estelle daily the last four weeks, spending time walking outside in the garden with her, or reading to her as she had been doing today. Jed popped in occasionally during those visits, as did her grandfather, and she had believed they were all doing a good job in convincing Estelle everything was all right between the three of them. Obviously she had been wrong!

She shook her head. 'If I've done anything to make you think that, then I—'

'Please, Georgie, don't think that I'm in any way criticising anything you've said or done these last weeks.' Grandie reached out and squeezed her hand reassuringly. 'I think you've been absolutely marvellous. And it can't have been easy for you, either, to keep up the pretence—'

'Grandie—'

'Please let me finish, dear,' Estelle interrupted gently. 'Georgie, the truth of the matter is, I'm very concerned about you; you don't look well.' She conveyed her concern.

The last four weeks had certainly been a strain, one Georgie had thought she wouldn't be able to get through at times. But Jed had helped in that by not being around too often when she visited Estelle, and her grandfather had also done his best not to be too visible.

But it had still been very hard to come here day after day, to keep up a bright and happy pose for Estelle—

when in reality her private life was falling apart. Was? It had already fallen apart!

'I've been working hard on the book—'

'You've been working hard on placating an old woman who ought to know better,' Estelle announced with her old indomitability. 'Georgie—' She broke off as the door to her sitting room was suddenly opened and Jed strode into the room, obviously having come here straight from the office, still wearing his business suit and snowy-white shirt.

Georgie literally felt her cheeks pale just at the sight of him. For one thing, no man had a right to be as attractive as Jed undoubtedly was. For another, if anything, her love for him had deepened over the last four weeks. As had her desire for him...

'Jed,' his grandmother greeted him warmly, holding out her hand for him to join the two women where they sat in chairs in the huge bay window that overlooked the garden. 'Georgie and I have just been having a little chat.'

'Well, I hope you don't mind, Grandie, but I would like to steal Georgie from you for a few minutes.' He smiled for his grandmother's benefit, but as his gaze passed over Georgie it felt as if she had been hit by a blast of icy cold air.

Was it any wonder, with Jed behaving like this, that Estelle had grown suspicious about this so-called reconciliation?

'Georgie is looking a little pale, don't you think?' Estelle prompted her grandson.

'Then a walk in the garden will do her the world of good,' Jed replied—without really replying at all.

Had he noticed the changes in Georgie the last few weeks? The fact that there were now shadows beneath her eyes, her cheeks were pale and hollow, that she had lost weight? From memory, Georgie knew that Jed hadn't looked at her enough to be aware of any of those things!

'Lovely.' She stood up, smiling brightly for Estelle's benefit—but inwardly wondering what on earth Jed had to say to her that necessitated their being alone together.

Because that was something both of them had avoided these last three weeks. Georgie, because of the embarrassed dismay she felt at the realisation of her love for him. And Jed—who knew how Jed thought or felt about anything…?

'Georgie, I want you to come back here and finish our conversation after you and Jed have finished talking,' Estelle called out to Georgie as she preceded Jed out of the room.

Jed turned to give his grandmother a chiding smile. 'Haven't you monopolised her enough for one day, Grandie?'

Estelle pouted across at him. 'You still aren't too big for me to reprimand, you know!'

'I do know.' Jed laughed softly. 'But I haven't seen Georgie all day,' he reasoned lightly.

'Take her out for dinner to make up for it,' Estelle suggested.

Jed glanced down at Georgie. 'I just might do that,' he agreed noncommittally.

Both of them knew he would make no such invitation, and that even if he did Georgie would refuse it.

Georgie turned to him in the hallway once he had

closed the door to Estelle's room. 'What is it?' she asked.

'The garden seems as good a place as any for us to talk,' Jed answered cryptically. 'Besides,' he continued as Georgie would have refused, 'Grandie might just be looking out for us there.'

Georgie turned abruptly to precede him down the hallway and stairs, her cheeks slightly pink as she remembered the last occasion he had said that Grandie might be looking at them, and Jed had kissed her.

But at least she felt as if she could breathe out in the garden; somehow any room in the house that contained Jed as well as herself was just too claustrophobic.

Jed wasted no time in coming to the point. 'I thought you would like to know that the deal with your boyfriend's father was just finalised,' he informed her disparagingly.

Georgie schooled her features to show no adverse reaction to this piece of news. Oh, she was glad that Gerald Lawson had received the money from the deal with the L & J Group that he needed to clear his debts. But Andrew was no longer her boyfriend…

There had simply been no way she could remain engaged to Andrew after she and Jed had made love together. No way she could ever think about marrying another man when she knew herself still irrevocably in love with her own ex-husband.

Her last meeting with Andrew, four weeks ago, had been painful to say the least. She had had to explain to him that she no longer intended marrying him, that their relationship was over.

Andrew had been devastated by her decision, couldn't

understand the reason for her sudden change of heart. In the circumstances—because she doubted that Sukie would keep quiet for ever where Jed's visit to Georgie's bedroom that evening was concerned!—Georgie had told Andrew as much of the truth as she felt necessary. That he had been stunned was putting it mildly.

Georgie thought Annabelle Lawson would not feel the same dismay at the broken engagement—she had probably wasted no time in producing the 'Lady-something-or-other' whom Jed had once mentioned as Annabelle's idea for Andrew's future wife!

But Georgie had hated having to hurt Andrew in the way that she undoubtedly had, and the last thing she felt in the mood for at the moment was Jed's derision where Andrew was concerned!

Her mouth quirked ruefully. 'What you're really trying to say, Jed, is that the L & J Group's deal with Gerald Lawson, for the purchase of some land he owned, has been finalised.'

'Am I?'

'Yes!' she assured him forcefully.

She had had no intention of telling Jed, or indeed anyone else, that her engagement to Andrew had been well and truly broken. Neither did she see why Gerald's deal with the L & J Group should be put in jeopardy just because she was no longer going to marry Andrew. By keeping up the pretence of a reconciliation in front of Estelle, Georgie considered she was keeping to her side of the bargain; there was no reason why Jed shouldn't be made to do the same.

Although, after the conversation she had just had with Estelle, she had the distinct feeling that one of them had definitely let the side down as regarded their supposed reconciliation!

'Whatever,' Jed said. 'The man has his money.'

'And you have your land,' she reasoned.

'The L & J Group has its land,' Jed corrected harshly. 'I don't appear to have anything!'

'Poor Jed,' Georgie derided unsympathetically.

'You—'

'You know, Jed, I think perhaps you ought to go up and have a quiet word with Estelle,' she interrupted. She knew from experience that exchanging barbed comments between the two of them was not going to achieve anything! 'She seems less than convinced by our so-called reconciliation,' she added thoughtfully.

'She doesn't?'

'Mmm,' Georgie replied. 'That's what she was talking to me about when you came in.'

'Damn,' he muttered with an irritable glance up at the window of his grandmother's room.

'No, "it's all your fault"? No, "you should have done better, Georgie"?' she taunted.

'Believe it or not, I don't consider you the fall-guy— or girl!—for everything that goes wrong in my life!' Jed's scowl deepened.

Georgie took the opportunity to note the changes in him over the last four weeks. The grey hair at his temples seemed more defined, his face thinner—and grimmer! Perhaps he had found the last four weeks a strain too?

'You surprise me,' she said with deliberate flippancy; she could not start feeling sorry for Jed. That way lay certain disaster! 'But perhaps it's time to tell Estelle the truth? She seems so much better, and—'

'And you're eager to get back to your fiancé!' Jed finished scathingly. 'No doubt the wedding plans need some working on too!'

'You—' She broke off her angry retort; if she lost her temper with him she might just say something she would later regret. And there was already enough for her to regret... 'I refuse to argue with you, Jed,' she told him calmly.

'Do you?' he responded challengingly.

'Yes,' she assured him determinedly. 'My suggestion that you tell Estelle the truth has nothing to do with— with Andrew.' She swallowed hard.

'Somehow I find that a little hard to believe,' Jed returned dryly.

'Somehow, Jed, I just don't care what you believe,' she rejoined. 'Estelle is obviously suspicious. I just think it would be better to tell her the truth now, and explain our reasons for the subterfuge, rather than let her find out later and be disappointed.'

'In me? Or you?' Jed prompted scathingly.

Georgie gave a weary sigh. 'In any of us. Grandfather was in on this too, remember?'

'So he was,' Jed agreed. 'You want me to go upstairs now and tell her? Is that it?' He looked grim at the prospect.

'Well, I think it might be better coming from you,' Georgie said slowly. 'I'll come back and see Estelle tomorrow, as usual, of course—'

'Oh, of course,' he grated.

'Look, Jed, either you can do it or I will,' she told

him. 'I just feel that the pretence has gone on long enough.'

He thrust his hands into his trouser pockets, turning away to look out over the extensive gardens, his shoulders hunched in thought.

Georgie let him think, knowing she was right about this. Estelle was a lot better, stronger, and wouldn't thank any of them for keeping up this pretence any longer than was necessary—would probably accuse them all of trying to make a fool of her if they did. In fact, if Georgie knew Estelle, the older woman would probably be thoroughly annoyed with all of them!

Finally Jed turned back to face Georgie, his expression grimmer than ever. 'Okay,' he agreed. 'I'll go up and talk to her. But I would appreciate your moral support, at least, when you visit her tomorrow.'

What he meant was that his grandmother was going to be angry with him anyway over the pretence, that he was going to need Georgie and her grandfather's support for what he had done!

'Of course,' Georgie assured him wearily, turning back towards the house.

'Oh, and Georgie...?' Jed called after her.

She turned back reluctantly. 'Yes?' she replied warily.

'Grandie is right,' he said. 'You don't look well.'

How did he expect her to look? Four weeks ago the two of them had made love. As a result of that she had broken off her engagement to Andrew. Worst of all, she had realised, despite all her attempts to bury the emotion, that she was still deeply in love with Jed!

She shrugged. 'I'm sure the last few weeks haven't been easy for any of us.'

Jed didn't look convinced by this explanation. 'How's the work going?'

She brightened slightly. 'Absolutely fine. I've just had my second book accepted.'

'That's good,' Jed agreed slowly, his gaze still focused on the paleness of her face. 'I don't suppose— No.' He stopped himself. 'Bad idea.'

'What is?' Georgie persisted.

He drew in a harsh breath. 'Grandie suggested the two of us had dinner together this evening. I just wondered— But I suppose you'll probably be out with Lawson this evening, celebrating your second literary success?'

Had she misunderstood, or was Jed really inviting her to have dinner with him tonight…?

A few minutes ago, when Grandie had made the suggestion, Georgie had thought the idea unacceptable to both of them—had been sure she would refuse even if Jed made such an offer. But now that he might actually be doing so…!

She shook her head, watching him warily. 'I have no plans to go anywhere this evening.'

Jed's eyes widened. 'You don't?'

'No,' she confirmed.

'I thought— Never mind what I thought,' he dismissed harshly. 'Georgie, would you allow me to buy you dinner this evening to celebrate the acceptance of your second book?'

Georgie stared at him, realising as she did so that this was the first time—ever!—that Jed had actually asked her out. Five years ago there had been no real courtship, just a proposal on her eighteenth birthday, and the two of them had never actually gone out together as such.

Oh, not that she thought Jed was inviting her out on a date this evening either, but it was certainly a novel experience!

She glanced across at Jed. His expression was guarded, as if he already knew what her answer was going to be—and was already prepared for her refusal!

'Dinner this evening would be lovely, thank you, Jed,' she accepted, holding back her smile as his eyes widened predictably with shocked surprise; he really had thought she was going to refuse!

His surprised expression turned to one of wary suspicion. 'You're really agreeing to go out to dinner with me...?' he pressed.

Georgie grinned at his obvious disbelief. 'If you're really asking me—yes!'

Why not? The last four weeks, apart from her visits to Grandie, had been spent mostly in her apartment; certainly she hadn't been out in the evening at all. Besides, it was worth accepting the invitation just to see Jed's uncharacteristic confusion. Although whether she would still feel that way at the end of the evening was another matter!

'Oh, I'm really asking,' he confirmed, straightening determinedly. 'I'll book a table somewhere for eight and call for you about seven-thirty, shall I?'

'Fine,' she accepted, avoiding looking at him now that the decision had been made. 'Now, I know that Estelle asked me to go up and see her again after the two of us had spoken together, but I really think it would be better if you went back alone. Tell her I will call back to see her tomorrow.' Georgie paused, then went on, 'She definitely knows something isn't right about this situation.'

And Georgie was already shaking enough from having accepted Jed's invitation to have dinner with him this evening. She didn't feel up to explaining things to Estelle as well!

Jed said, 'I'll talk to her.'

'Right, then,' Georgie agreed, not quite sure how to take her leave now that it had come to it. 'I'll see you later.' She turned away, ready to leave.

'Georgie…?'

She came to a halt as Jed called her name, turning slowly back to face him. 'Yes?' she responded uncertainly.

His eyes blazed deeply silver. 'Thank you.'

Georgie wasn't at all sure what he was thanking her for.

'Seven-thirty,' he confirmed.

'Yes…' she said.

He gave a slight smile. 'I'm looking forward to it.'

'Good,' Georgie returned, before turning and hurrying away, completely unable to return the sentiment—because she had no idea how she felt about going out to dinner with Jed!

That she loved him she didn't doubt. That she desired him she also had no doubt. That Jed definitely felt the latter, if not the former, she also had no doubt after their time together four weeks ago.

But was that enough for them to even get through an evening together, let alone anything else…?

CHAPTER TWELVE

By THE time seven-thirty came around Georgie had worked herself up into such a state of nervous tension that she almost felt as if she was going to faint!

What on earth had she thought she was doing earlier, accepting an invitation to go out to dinner with Jed, of all people? Of all men!

She hadn't been able to resist, came the unhesitant reply.

Not that she had had too much time to reflect and berate herself in the last three hours. She had gone to the telephone half a dozen times with the intention of ringing Jed at her grandfather's, to tell him she couldn't make it after all. She'd gone through her wardrobe an equal amount of times, trying on outfit after outfit and deciding she didn't look or feel good in any of them. In short, she was a nervous wreck. A hot and bothered nervous wreck, at that.

She had lost weight during the last few weeks, and yet none of her clothes fitted her properly—too tight in some places, and too loose in others. The plain black dress she had finally settled on—having gone back to one of the first things she had tried on!—didn't feel right either. But as she had run out of time, it would just have to do.

Her face was hot and flushed, and no amount of make-up could hide the dark smudges beneath her eyes caused by lack of sleep. Her lip-gloss didn't seem to want to go on straight either, and her hair—freshly washed—seemed to have a will of its own that included standing up on end in places!

But it was too late to worry about all of those things now, because Jed was already in the lift on his way up to her apartment!

'You look lovely,' Jed told her appreciatively as she met him coming out of the lift.

Georgie just couldn't help it—she burst out laughing.

'Was it something I said?' Jed gave a quizzical smile at her response, looking very handsome and self-assured in a black dinner suit and snowy white shirt.

'I'm having a bad hair day.' She gave a rueful shake of her head as she reached out to lightly clasp his arm and draw him into her apartment. 'As well as a bad make-up day and a my-clothes-don't-fit-me day,' she exclaimed. 'It must be so much easier for men—you just take a shower, put on your dinner clothes, and you're ready to go!'

'You think?' Jed grinned.

Georgie gave him a considering look. He did look absolutely wonderful in his dinner clothes, his hair slightly damp from the shower he must have taken—and he smelt gorgeous too.

'I think,' she finally confirmed. 'Would you like a drink before we go?' She indicated the bottle of white wine she had opened earlier, having drunk a glass herself in the hope that it would steady her nerves. She had obviously been wrong—she was so nervous now her hands were shaking!

'Thanks.' Jed accepted the offer, unbuttoning his

jacket before sitting down in one of the armchairs. 'In the face of your own admissions, I feel it only fair to tell you that I cut myself shaving, tried on two other shirts, also white, before settling on this one, decided I need to go up a size in a dinner suit—and sprayed shaving foam under my arms instead of deodorant!'

Georgie turned to stare at him, arrested in the action of pouring his glass of white wine. Surely Jed wasn't as nervous as she was about the two of them having dinner together…? Somehow the words 'Jed' and 'nervous' just didn't go together!

'You're just trying to make me feel better,' she said as she handed him his glass of wine.

He raised dark brows. 'I forgot to mention that originally I also put on one black sock and one brown one, only discovering my mistake when I came to put on my shoes,' he elaborated self-derisively.

Maybe he wasn't just trying to make her feel better, after all…

Although Georgie still refused to believe it would have been the thought of dinner with her that had caused this uncharacteristic behavior.

Of course it wasn't!

'Was your chat with Grandie that bad?' she prompted as she sat down in the chair opposite his.

'My chat with— Ah,' he nodded. 'Would you mind if we talked about that later?'

'Not at all.' She shrugged, sipping her wine, and almost choking on it at Jed's next words.

'I've booked a table for us at Fabio's,' he told her.

Their favourite restaurant! Well…perhaps that was too intimate a description for the Italian restaurant he had just mentioned, but they had certainly frequented that particular restaurant often during their marriage— had celebrated their wedding anniversaries there too. All three of them!

'Are you okay?' Jed queried, sitting forward to look at Georgie concernedly as she coughed slightly, some of her wine having gone down the wrong way.

'Fine,' she told him shakily, putting down her wine glass before standing up. 'Perhaps we had better be on our way.'

'There's no rush,' Jed assured her as he stood up to hold her red jacket for her to put on. 'Fabio was so pleased to hear from us that he told me he's going to keep our usual table for us.'

To hear from 'us'... Their 'usual table'...

Georgie was taken aback. 'But surely you've been back there in the two years since—since—?'

'Since the two of us parted?' Jed finished softly. 'No. As I just said, it's our restaurant. It wouldn't have been right to take anyone else there. Besides—'

'Besides...?' Georgie pressed, looking at him from beneath lowered lashes as the two of them descended in the lift.

He looked at the elevator's ceiling. 'Something else we can talk about later.'

There seemed to be an awful lot of things they were going to discuss later: his earlier conversation with Grandie, and now this.

Oh, well, at least they would have something to talk about rather than just sitting looking at each other all evening!

*   *   *

'I feel a complete fraud,' Georgie said, glancing uncomfortably around the restaurant after Fabio himself had escorted them to their table, personally seeing her seated opposite Jed before snapping his fingers imperiously for the waiter to come and take their drinks order.

None of the other diners appeared to be taking any undue interest in them, but, as Georgie knew from visits here in the past, it wasn't the done thing to appear interested in your fellow eaters.

She turned back to Jed. 'Fabio is obviously under the impression we're once again a couple,' she observed awkwardly.

Jed looked at her. 'It doesn't matter what he may or may not think—does it?'

No, not really. She just wasn't comfortable with it.

'Thank you.' She smiled up at the waiter as he poured some wine into a glass for her.

'You know, Georgie,' Jed said slowly once they were alone again, sitting forward in his seat to look across the table at her, 'you really aren't looking well. Perhaps you should see a doctor?'

She raised auburn brows. 'I thought you said earlier that I look lovely,' she reminded him dryly.

'You do,' he confirmed impatiently. 'It's just—'

'Jed, I just need to eat,' she assured him, deliberately burying her nose in the menu so that she didn't have to look at him.

She was determined to enjoy this evening. She knew that very soon her visits to Estelle would have to come to an end, which meant that her occasional meetings with Jed would be over. This evening might be all she would see of him for some time...

'I'm going to have the avocado vinaigrette and Dover sole,' she decided, before closing the menu. 'How about you?' she questioned conversationally.

Jed closed his own menu. 'I'll have the same as you. Georgie—'

'Shall we drink a toast to Estelle's full recovery?' She held up her wine glass.

Jed looked irritated by her interruption. 'Very well,' he agreed, lightly touching his glass against hers.

The wine barely touched Georgie's lips before she replaced her glass down on the table. 'She is so much better, isn't she?' she said thankfully.

Jed's expression hardened. 'Eager to get back to your fiancé, Georgie?'

She met his gaze unblinkingly. 'About as eager as you must be to get back to your own life,' she returned noncommittally.

'I—' He broke off as the waiter arrived at their table to take their order, giving the other man a hard stare. 'Two avocado vinaigrettes, and two Dover—'

'I've changed my mind about the main course,' Georgie cut in lightly. 'I think I'll have the lamb noisettes instead of the Dover sole.' She smiled up at the waiter in apology. 'A woman's prerogative,' she told Jed humorously as he looked at her once the waiter had made a discreet exit.

'So I believe,' Jed acknowledged. 'Does Lawson know that you're having dinner with me this evening?' His voice had hardened noticeably.

'No,' Georgie answered without hesitation.

Once Andrew had calmed down, after she'd broken their engagement, the two of them had talked more rationally and had agreed that they would remain friends. But Georgie already knew that the friendship would consist of them being polite to each other if they should happen to meet by chance. It was very sad, and she really was sorry to lose Andrew's warmth and kindness from her life, but she also knew she had had no other choice.

Jed was watching her from between narrowed lids. 'Do you intend telling him?'

'No,' Georgie stated flatly.

'Why not?'

'Because it has no bearing on our relationship.' Their now non-existent-relationship…

'Georgie—'

'Jed, couldn't we just enjoy this evening? There's really no need to complicate things by talking about Andrew or—or anyone else you may have in your own life at the moment.'

Despite having had lunch with Sukie Lawson, Jed obviously wasn't too taken with the other woman. But that didn't mean there wasn't some other woman in his life…

Unpleasant though that thought might be!

'Unlike you, I don't have anyone else in my life,' Jed bit out harshly. 'At the moment, or at any other time!'

Georgie's eyes widened. His tone was too vehement for it to be anything other than the truth. But in that case *why* didn't Jed have someone in his life…?

'Georgie, you just don't get it, do you?' he continued, sitting forward in his chair as he did so.

Didn't get what? She—

She sat back in her seat as their first course was placed in front of them. 'This looks delicious,' she approved as she began to eat, and the moment—whatever it might have been!—passed. Jed picked up his knife and fork and also began to eat, albeit uninterestedly.

'This is very good,' Georgie murmured after several minutes' silence—a silence that was becoming more and more awkward while Jed only picked at his food rather than eating it. Her own appetite was rapidly waning too, in the face of Jed's brooding distraction. 'I wonder why it is that food always tastes better in a restaurant than when you've prepared it at home? Probably for that very reason.' She gave the answer herself seconds later, as none seemed to be forthcoming from Jed. 'After shopping for the food, and then spending time preparing and cooking it, I've usually lost interest by the time it comes to—'

'Georgie—stop it!' Jed cut in forcefully, grey eyes opaquely silver as he glared across the table at her. 'Just stop it!' he ordered, putting down his knife and fork and pushing his plate away as he gave up any pretence of eating his food. 'We aren't strangers out on a first date together! You don't have to make to make meaningless conversation to fill in any awkward silences!'

Making meaningless conversation...? Was that what she was doing? Probably. But the silence between them *had* been awkward!

'I'm sorry,' she apologised, pushing away her own plate, with most of the avocado uneaten. 'Maybe this wasn't such a good idea after all—'

'Of course it was a good idea!' Jed rasped. 'I just—' He reached across the table and clasped one of her hands between both of his. 'Georgie, do you have any idea how much I've longed to spend time with you like this? How much I—?'

'Jed, stop it!' She was the one to cry out now, staring at him with shocked eyes as she pulled her hand away from his, ignoring the tingling sensation she felt just from his touch. 'There's no audience—at least none that matters,' she amended, for the restaurant was packed with people. 'You don't have anyone to put on an act for now—certainly not me!—so—'

'I'm not putting on an act,' he grated, a nerve pulsing in his jaw. 'Damn it, Georgie, don't you know—have you never realised—just how much I—?'

'Is everything all right for you, Mr Lord?'

Georgie felt quite sorry for Fabio when his polite enquiry received a fiercely angry glare from Jed. The restaurant proprietor took an involuntary step back as Jed's gaze narrowed on him furiously.

'You—'

'Everything is wonderful.' Georgie cut in on what she was sure was going to be Jed's impolite reply. 'Thank you, Fabio.' She smiled again, to take the sting out of her own obvious dismissal of the restaurateur. 'How much you what, Jed?' She reminded them of their interrupted conversation once they were alone again, not sure she wanted to hear the answer to that question, but knowing she had to ask it nonetheless.

He closed his eyes briefly, at the same time drawing in a harshly controlling breath. 'You were right in your suspicions earlier concerning Grandie,' he said starkly. 'In fact, I would go one step further and say that you were more than right. Grandie admitted to me earlier this evening that she has always known that there was no reconciliation between us, that it was all a pretence!'

Georgie stared at him uncomprehendingly. 'I don't understand.'

'She was seriously ill when I told her the two of us had reconciled,' Jed explained, his expression grim. 'And that certainly was a factor in her initial recovery. But apparently she has known since seeing the two of us together again that there really was no reconciliation, that it was all an act.'

'I— You— But it's been weeks now!' Georgie gasped incredulous. 'And if she's known all this time why didn't she just say so and put an end to all this subterfuge?'

Jed pursed his lips. 'For the same reason I told her the lie in the first place. For the same reason I didn't just telephone you and tell you Grandie wanted to see you, but sought you out at the Lawsons' home instead. For the same reason I've wanted to hit Andrew Lawson every time I've seen the two of you together. For the same reason I had lunch with Sukie Lawson—'

'You aren't making any sense, Jed!' Georgie burst in emotionally. 'None of those things are related to each other—'

'Of course they're related!' he protested impatiently.

'No—'

'*Yes!*' Jed hissed fiercely, the nerve in his jaw beating a wild tattoo now. 'They are completely, one hundred per cent related—when you take into account the fact that I love you! That I have *always* loved you!'

Georgie could only stare at him.

And continue to stare…

CHAPTER THIRTEEN

FINALLY—when it seemed Jed was going to add nothing to that ludicrous statement!—Georgie drew in a deep breath before she answered him. 'Have you been drinking, Jed?' she asked suspiciously. 'Oh, I don't mean now,' she said, as his gaze flickered to his almost untouched glass of wine. 'Before. Maybe that was the reason you were so confused earlier when dressing—'

'I have not been drinking. Either now or earlier,' he stated firmly.

'But—'

'Georgie, is it really so difficult to believe that I love you?' he pleaded.

'Difficult?' she echoed. 'The very idea is ridiculous!'

His gaze remained unwavering on her face. 'Why is it?'

'Because—' She drew in a deeply controlling breath. 'Jed, even if it were true—'

'It is,' he assured her sincerely.

'Even if it were true,' she repeated firmly, 'how can you possibly equate such a claim with taking Sukie Lawson out to lunch?'

Let's see him get himself out of that one! Jed might claim he hadn't been drinking earlier this evening, but there was certainly something very wrong with him. How could he possibly claim to love her. It just didn't make sense!

169

In fact, this whole evening was starting to take on a dream-like quality—or did she mean nightmarish?

'I had hoped to make you jealous,' Jed admitted.

He had succeeded! Georgie could still clearly remember her feelings that day when she'd learnt that Jed was going out with Sukie, and it wasn't a pleasant memory. She had wanted to hit Sukie, and scream and shout at Jed!

'The same jealousy I feel towards Andrew Lawson,' he continued harshly. 'Every time his name is so much as mentioned I want to hit something! And as for thinking of the two of you together—'

'Jed, Andrew and I don't have that sort of relationship,' Georgie shot in. She wanted no misunderstandings on that point; this situation was already complicated enough!

She still couldn't accept anything of what Jed was saying to her. They had been married for three years, for goodness' sake, and not once during that time had Jed ever told her that he loved her. Unless he had discovered these feelings since the two of them had parted? But, no, hadn't he just claimed to have *always* loved her...?

'Jed—'

'Are you telling me that you and Lawson aren't— physically involved?' Jed cut across what she had been about to say.

Her cheeks coloured hotly. 'I don't have to tell you anything about my relationship with Andrew—'

'But you just did,' Jed reasoned determinedly.

Yes, she had. And she wished that she hadn't. 'Jed, I'm not sure we should be having this conversation at all—let alone in the middle of a busy restaurant.'

'I disagree. Oh, not about the location,' he conceded dryly as the waiter discreetly removed their used plates. 'But I think the conversation itself is long overdue. Five years overdue, to be exact.'

Five years... They had married each other five years ago...

But they had parted again three years later, she reminded herself. Because Jed hadn't loved her. Because he'd been involved with another woman. She might have been naïve two years ago, but even she had known that wasn't the behaviour of a man in love with his wife!

She shook her head sadly. 'Jed, nothing has changed in the last two years—'

'I disagree,' he rejoined. '*You've* changed. Your grandfather warned me that you were too young when we married, that you needed a few more years to grow up, to enjoy your freedom. But I wasn't willing to wait—'

'I may have been young, Jed, but even I knew that there had to be something seriously wrong with your marriage when your husband was publicly having an affair with another woman!' she burst out.

'When I *what*!' Jed exclaimed.

'Mia Douglas,' she reminded.

'Mia Douglas...?' he repeated, his expression blank.

Georgie felt the sting of tears in her eyes. Had Jed's relationship with the other woman been so unimportant to him that he even had trouble remembering it now? That same relationship that had blown her own world apart?

Or was it just that he had never realised she had known about his affair with the actress?

When Jed had returned from his so-called business trip two years ago it had been to find Georgie, and her belongings, removed from their apartment. When he'd finally tracked her down to the hotel where she was staying she had refused to discuss anything with him, except to tell him that she had made a mistake, that their marriage was over. Oh, he had argued, and cajoled, but to no avail. Georgie had remained adamant in her decision.

That had been when Jed had really lost it—demanding to know if there were someone else in her life, if she were seeing another man!

Georgie had then thrown his own motive back in his face by telling him she had only married him at all to please her grandfather, but that her inability to have children now made that arrangement null and void, and their marriage was well and truly over.

How dared he now pretend he didn't even remember his affair with Mia Douglas?

'Mia Douglas, Jed,' she said tightly. 'Surely you remember her? Tall. Blonde. Beautiful. A charity dinner you attended with her in Los Angeles?'

'I've never been to Los Angeles,' he responded. 'And to my knowledge I've only ever met Mia Douglas once. She was attending some dinner or other being given at our hotel in Hawaii one time when I was there, and a damned nuisance the whole thing was too, with photographers all over the place disturbing the other guests—' He broke off, his gaze narrowed as he looked at Georgie suspiciously. 'Georgie, you aren't telling me that you left me two years ago because of some damned publicity photograph of Mia Douglas and myself that somehow found its way into the English newspapers?'

Georgie could barely breathe. A pain in her chest seemed to constrict her airway.

Was she saying that? Had she been mistaken all this time? Had there been no reason for her to leave Jed after all?

But of course there had been a reason, she instantly berated herself. Jed hadn't married her because he loved her, but because it had been yet another business merger on behalf of the Lord and Jones families. That was the real truth of the matter. Jed's supposed involvement with another woman was merely a side issue—a side issue! At the time she had thought she might die from the pain of seeing Jed with another woman…!

But she hadn't died, and in the last two years she had grown much stronger as a person. She was successful in her own right, completely independent financially. Nothing Jed said now could change any of that.

She straightened. 'I left you two years ago, Jed, because our marriage was over. If it ever really began!' she added scathingly, before picking up her evening bag and standing up. 'Just as I am leaving now. If you'll excuse me?' she told him pleasantly, and turned away.

The first she knew of Jed following her was when she emerged out onto the street and found him standing beside her. She wished he hadn't—because she wasn't sure how much longer she could hold back her tears!

'I'm driving you home, Georgie,' he told her firmly, before she could utter a word.

She glanced back at the brightly lit restaurant. 'Fabio—'

'I've made our apologies and settled the bill,' Jed explained grimly. 'Being the romantic that he is, Fabio probably thinks I'm whisking you away early so that the two of us can spend the rest of the evening making love together.'

'That only increased our problems the last time we did that!' Georgie returned waspishly.

Jed shot her a sharp look. 'What do you mean?'

Georgie avoided that searching gaze. 'Nothing,' she said. 'I really don't need you to drive me home, Jed—'

'*I* need to drive you home,' he decided. 'Let me at least have the peace of mind of knowing you got there safely, hmm?' he encouraged hardly, before reaching into his pocket for his keys and unlocking the car.

'I've managed to achieve that for the last two years without any help from you,' she told him.

His mouth tightened at her deliberate barb, but he made no reply, simply opened the passenger door pointedly for her to get inside the car.

Georgie just wanted to get away, to be on her own. But at the same time she didn't feel like continuing this stand up verbal fight with Jed to achieve it...

'Oh, okay!' she accepted, before getting into the car, her face averted from his when he got in beside her seconds later.

But he didn't start the engine, instead turned to her in the semi-darkness of the interior of the car. 'Georgie, for me, making love with you four weeks ago was like dying and going to heaven,' he said.

She trembled, not sure how much longer she would be able to hold on to her emotions.

This was hard, so much harder than she could ever have imagined.

How could she go on fighting him if he said things like that to her?

But she had to! There was no going back now, only forwards. And that future didn't—couldn't!—include Jed.

'I love you, Georgie.'

No...! Not now! All that time, all those years she had yearned— She couldn't—

'I've loved you since the moment I first saw you,' he continued huskily. 'You were like the little sister I had never had. Eight years old, all arms, legs and eyes, weighed down by a long mane of copper-coloured hair,' he recalled affectionately.

'And I worshipped the ground you walked on!' Georgie remembered self-disgustedly.

Jed smiled. 'If by that you mean that you accepted me unconditionally, then, yes, I suppose that's true. You were the first person who ever had.'

'Estelle—'

'Loved me,' he acknowledged. 'But not unconditionally. I was the son of the daughter who had so let her down—'

'She let you down too!' Georgie defended, only able to guess at what it must have felt like to be abandoned by your own mother in the way that Jed had been.

'Yes.' He sighed. 'But don't you see? Estelle was always looking for signs of that emotional instability in me, was never sure that I would still be around once I was an adult. Whereas you—' he smiled again '—you always expected me to keep my promises. I honestly don't think it ever occurred to you to doubt that I would. Heady stuff, Georgie. By the time you were eighteen I was completely under your spell, totally and utterly in love with you.'

She swallowed hard. 'But you never said those words to me…!' she remembered achingly.

'I didn't dare,' Jed confessed. 'My mother walked out on me when I was four years old. My grandmother, although she loved me, kept me slightly at arm's length, always waiting for the day I would just disappear.' He sighed shakily. 'I didn't dare tell you how much I love you, Georgie! I—I was frightened to tell you—thought the hurt would be less if you ever left me. I was wrong,' he added heavily.

She could see how it might appear that way to Jed, how much his mother walking out on him as a child must have damaged his trust in any other woman who claimed to love him. But at the same time she was afraid herself—so afraid—to believe what he was telling her. Because if she did—

'And I suppose this declaration of love has absolutely nothing to do with your "arrangement" with my grandfather?' she reminded him accusingly.

'You mentioned that two years ago… I had no idea what you were talking about then, and even less so now! The only agreement I had with your grandfather five years ago was that I wouldn't swamp you with the love I felt for you, that I would give you time to grow up, to reach your full potential, in whatever direction that might lie. Of course, I hoped it would still be as my wife, but…' He sighed. 'You've obviously achieved your ambition these last two years without me.'

Yes, she had, but— 'I could still have done that as your wife,' she told him softly. 'I—my grandfather seemed to think our marriage was a business arrangement?' But she was less forceful in the accusation now, less sure of herself, and wondered if she could possibly—just possibly—have misunderstood what her grandfather had said two years ago.

'Definitely not,' Jed denied. 'Damn it, Georgie, if you really believe that I'll give up all claim on the Lord & Jones Group—branch out on my own!'

'You would really do that?'

He nodded. 'I'm not saying it would be easy, but—yes. If it means that you would believe me once and for all when I tell you I love you, that's exactly what I'll do! Without you, Georgie—' his voice broke slightly '—my life has no meaning anyway.'

Georgie couldn't believe he was saying these things. And meaning them! Because she could tell by the grim determination of his expression that he *did* mean them.

'My lifetime ambition is to be with you, Georgie.' He reminded her of the accusation she had thrown at him four weeks ago. 'To just love you and be with you,' he emphasised clearly.

She needed time—not too much time!—but some time to fully take in the things Jed had said to her this evening. Most of all she needed time to accept that he really did love her, that he always had!

'Could you drive me home now, please, Jed?' she requested evenly.

'I—'

'Please?' she requested again intensely.

He looked at her for a long time, and then he nodded abruptly. 'Of course,' he acceded tautly, switching on the car engine at last to begin the journey back to her apartment.

Georgie leant back in her seat, her eyes closed, desperately trying to make sense of the things Jed had said to her this evening and finally concluding that the only thing that did make sense was that he loved her! And the 'arrangement' between her grandfather and Jed had only been made at all because the older man had been aware of just how deeply Jed loved her. He had feared for her own personality in the face of such intense love, and it was her grandfather's own love for her that had prompted him to ask Jed to proceed with caution where she was concerned.

Jed loved her...!

Had always loved her.

Would always love her.

Did she really need to know anything else? The answer to that was a definite no!

But there were some confessions of her own she still had to make. She wondered what Jed's response would be to at least one of them...

CHAPTER FOURTEEN

'WOULD you like to come in for coffee?' Georgie offered shyly once Jed had parked his car outside her apartment building.

'I would love to come in,' he confirmed. 'But I never drink coffee at this time of night.'

'That's okay,' she assured him as she got out of the car. 'Neither do I!'

And her invitation had nothing to do with offering Jed a cup of coffee. They still had so many things to talk about. But all of them were based on her accepting the possibility that Jed might really have been in love with her all this time. Something she still found a little hard to believe.

'Georgie—'

'Let's just go upstairs, hmm, Jed?' she suggested, waiting for him to get out of the car and accompany her.

They didn't speak on their way through the reception area, or as they went up in the lift together. But Georgie could feel the tension between them, knew that Jed was as nervous about the outcome of the next few minutes as she was.

She kicked off her shoes the moment they entered the apartment, turning to raise questioning brows at Jed as she heard him make a sound behind her.

'It's been years since I've seen you do that,' he told her gruffly. 'You always used to kick off your shoes the moment we came home from an evening out,' he explained at her puzzled look.

'Oh, dear.' Georgie grimaced, could feel the warmth of embarrassment in her cheeks. It wasn't a habit she had ever been aware of. But obviously Jed had... 'How irritating for you,' she said.

Jed looked at her unblinkingly. 'Georgie, nothing you do has ever irritated me. Or ever could,' he added softly.

Georgie turned away from the intensity of that silver gaze. 'As you don't want coffee, can I offer you a glass of whisky?'

'No, thanks.' He sat down in one of the armchairs. 'I would rather be stone-cold sober when I receive the executioner's sentence.'

'The—? Don't be silly, Jed,' she responded. 'You mentioned earlier that Grandie had deliberately kept up the subterfuge about our reconciliation? Does she know that you—that you—'

'That I love you?' Jed finished dryly. 'Of course. The only one who has never been aware of it seems to be you, Georgie.'

Because she had been very young when they'd married five years ago. And very immature. An older woman might possibly have seen Jed's reticence concerning actually saying the words 'I love you' for exactly what it was—the only self-protection he had left!

'I see,' she said. 'I've been extremely stupid, haven't I, Jed?'

She closed her eyes briefly. 'Stupid and selfish. I was so confused by the time my grandfather mentioned some sort of an arrangement between the two of you two years ago that I completely misunderstood and thought I had merely been part of a business deal. And I've refused to speak to Grandfather for the last two years because of that misunderstanding.

'I'm sure if you explain—'

'I'm going to do more than that,' she assured him, tears shimmering in her eyes. 'All this time he was only trying to protect me—as he always had! When I see him tomorrow I will offer him my most humble apologies for ever doubting him.'

Jed gave her a sympathetic smile. 'I'm sure he will appreciate that.'

Which brought them back—inevitably—to the situation between Jed and herself...

'Jed, you asked me earlier what I was going to tell Andrew about having had dinner with you this evening—'

'And you, very rightly, told me to mind my own business,' he drawled ruefully.

'I'm not under any obligation to tell Andrew anything any more,' she confessed uncomfortably. 'Jed, I—I broke my engagement to Andrew four weeks ago!'

'Four weeks ago—!' He straightened in the chair, his expression watchful now. 'But—'

'The day after the two of us had made love.' She confirmed the conclusion she could see dawning in his expression.

'Why?' he prompted.

'Well, for one thing it would have been very wrong not to. For another...' She hesitated, a small part of past hurts still lingering. But Jed had bared his soul to her this evening, the least she could do was to be truthful about her own feelings towards him. 'Jed, when we married five years ago I was deeply in love with you—'

'I know that,' he groaned achingly. 'I was just always so frightened of losing you that I didn't dare tell you I felt the same way. I had hoped that I showed you how I felt when we made love—'

'You did,' she assured him undoubtingly; maturity had helped her to see that was exactly what he had done. As he had four weeks ago when they made love together again... 'You said earlier that I've changed the last two years.'

'You have,' he responded admiringly.

'One thing about me has—has never changed, Jed,' she continued more assuredly. 'I loved you five years ago and I love you now. If anything, I love you more now than I did then!' The words just burst out of her, as if she had to say them before she lost her nerve. 'I didn't just break my engagement to Andrew because the two of us had made love together. I also broke it because I could never marry one man while being deeply in love with another.'

'Me...?' Jed's voice was so low it was barely discernible. A nerve pulsed erratically in the hardness of his cheek.

'You,' she went on warmly. 'Oh, Jed, I love you so much,' she told him, going down on her knees beside his chair to take one of his hands in hers. 'I love you,' she said again, that emotion shining in the brightness of her eyes.

Jed gathered her up into his arms, gazing at her wonderingly for several seconds before his mouth moved to gently claim hers.

Love. It had been there all the time. In Jed's every touch. Every kiss. The difference between now and five years ago was that she knew it with every fibre of her being.

'Will you marry me?' Jed breathed when at last he raised his head to look at her with dark eyes.

'Oh, yes,' she accepted without hesitation. 'And let's make it soon, hmm?' she encouraged throatily.

Jed's arms tightened about her. 'I want it to be different this time, Georgie. I want to give you an old-fashioned courtship—take you out, send you flowers, leave you in no doubt as to how I feel about you—'

'I think I could stand a week or two of that.' She nodded, eyes sparkling mischievously. 'But no longer, hmm?'

He smoothed the hair at her temples, his hand shaking slightly. 'I don't want to rush you into anything, Georgie,' he explained. 'This time you have to be very sure—because once you're my wife again I will never let you go! I only let you go last time because your grandfather advised me that by letting you go you might one day come back.'

Georgie could see the logic in that—even if it hadn't exactly worked out that way! What a shock the announcement of her engagement to Andrew must have been for all of them...

'I don't ever want to leave you again,' she assured Jed with certainty. 'I love you, Jed. I always will. But I also think it might be nice for our son or daughter if we are actually remarried before they're born. Don't you?' she encouraged.

'Our son or daughter…?' Jed repeated, looking at her uncomprehendingly.

'You told me earlier today that I don't look well, that I ought to see a doctor,' she reminded him happily. 'I've already seen one. Two days ago. He confirmed that I am going to have a baby. Our baby, Jed,' she told him emotionally. 'Our million to one chance is a fact—and due to be born in eight months!'

'But— I— You—'

She laughed happily at his totally dazed expression. 'It's true, Jed,' she assured him lovingly. 'We're pregnant!'

Emotions flitted rapidly across his usually guarded face: disbelief, doubt, hope, and finally, as Georgie continued to smile at him with ecstatic certainty, complete wonder.

'I can't believe it!' he gasped at last.

'Neither could I to start with,' she admitted, unable to stop smiling, it seemed. 'But the doctor has assured me that there is no mistake.'

She had gone to the doctor initially because she really hadn't been feeling well: nauseous, dizzy occasionally, with her appetite extremely erratic. When the doctor had calmly announced she had all those symptoms because she was pregnant, Georgie had almost fallen off her chair, asking him if he was sure. A simple test had only confirmed his diagnosis.

Georgie had been walking around in a seventh heaven for the last two days, torn between euphoria that she was at last to have Jed's baby and despair because she couldn't share it with him. But now she could!

'It really is true, Jed,' she told him. 'My sudden

change to lamb for dinner this evening?' she reminded him. 'That was because the thought of fish suddenly made me feel ill. I'm pregnant, Jed, and I couldn't be happier!' Her smile was radiant.

Jed still looked totally dazed, staring at her as if he couldn't believe she were quite real.

Georgie snuggled against him reassuringly; after all, she had had forty-eight hours longer than he had to get used to the idea, and she still pinched herself occasionally to see if she wasn't dreaming.

'I can't wait to see Grandfather's face when we tell him we're going to make him a great-grandfather!' she said mischievously; perhaps the news might help alleviate, in part, some of the hurt she must have caused him when she wouldn't even see him these last two years…! 'Would you like a boy or a girl, Jed?' She looked up at him quizzically.

He swallowed hard, his eyes glistening. 'I really don't care which it is—as long as you're both healthy,' he finally managed. 'But if it's a boy it certainly won't be called Jeremiah!'

Georgie giggled happily. 'I'm sorry I teased you about your name that evening.' She grinned. 'But I'm sure we'll be able to think of something a little more attractive than both our names. After all, we have eight months to think of it!'

Jed's arms tightened about her. 'And a lifetime together to enjoy! I really do love you very much, Georgie. And I intend saying that often in the future.'

Strange, now that she knew Jed loved her, the words no longer seemed necessary…

But at the same time there was a certain joy in the freedom of at last saying those words to each other.

A joy that Georgie had no doubts would last for a lifetime. Their lifetime together.

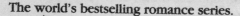

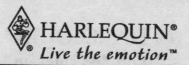

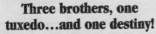

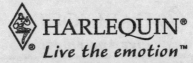

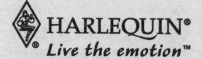

The world's bestselling romance series.

HARLEQUIN®
Presents

Seduction and Passion Guaranteed!

Your dream ticket to the vacation of a lifetime!

Why not relax and allow Harlequin Presents® to whisk you away to stunning international locations with our new miniseries...

FOREIGN AFFAIRS

Where irresistible men and sophisticated women surrender to seduction under the golden sun.

Don't miss this opportunity to experience glamorous lifestyles and exotic settings in:

Robyn Donald's
THE TEMPTRESS OF TARIKA BAY
on sale July, #2336

THE FRENCH COUNT'S MISTRESS
by Susan Stephens
on sale August, #2342

THE SPANIARD'S WOMAN
by Diana Hamilton
on sale September, #2346

THE ITALIAN MARRIAGE
by Kathryn Ross
on sale October, #2353

FOREIGN AFFAIRS... A world full of passion!

Pick up a Harlequin Presents® novel and you will enter a world of spine-tingling passion and provocative, tantalizing romance!

Available wherever Harlequin books are sold.

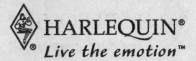

HARLEQUIN®
Live the emotion™

Visit us at www.eHarlequin.com

HPFAMA